L. M. VANGALEN

Within the Silence

Book Two in The Chronicles of Azarathe

First edition

ISBN: 978-1-7775469-1-5

This book was professionally typeset on Reedsy.
Find out more at reedsy.com

*There are always people in your life who influence you,
whether or not they are aware of the impact.*

*With thanks to my family and friends who kept
pushing me to finish the book and get it out there.*

*There are many things yet to see, people I have yet to meet,
and so much more to learn.*

May my journey inspire you to write about your own journey.

Preface

Sometimes I think it would be nice to get lost in the space between time. When you are not where you were but are not yet where you are going. Where the infinitely possible is laid out before you and you have but to choose a path, a direction, a destination.

Here We Go Again

Beep….. Beep….. Beep…..

Slowly becoming aware of my surroundings, I sense I'm not out of danger yet. Focus, damn it! Focus!

Focus on what? Oh, yeah. Breathing. That's a good place to start. Breathe in. Ouch. Damn it. Broken ribs again. Breathe out. Take it slow. Breathe in. Breathe out. Keep going…..

Beep….. Beep….. Beep…..

Fighting against the blackness, I realize I had faded out again. This time-jumping shit has got to stop. Can we turn off the alarm clock, please?! Damn, that's annoying.

Wait, a minute…..

Beep….. Beep…Beep…Beep.. Beep. Beep.Beep.Beeeeeeeeeep……

"She's crashing! Get the doctor!"

Uh oh. That doesn't sound good.

"Clear!"

—- SNAP —-

Fuck! That hurt! Hey, I was crashing???

"We've got rhythm. Let's get her into the ICU!"

—- Jesus H Christ, I feel like I'm on fire. Breathe, damn it, breathe…

"Looks stable. Ms. Kennedy, the blood work should be ready shortly. Find me if anything changes." I heard the snap of latex as the doctor removed her gloves.

"Yes, Dr. Kelvin," the nurse replied. "Ms. Andrews, let's get those IV lines hooked up and our patient comfortable."

Hold on. Hooked up to what? Oh, hell no — Nurse, scan my arm!! Dear God on Earth, scan my arm! Wake the fuck up, Sleeping Beauty or this is going to be a really short lifetime!

Beep…. Beep…. Beep….

As my eyes slowly respond to my request and light briefly filters through my lashes, I tried to assess where I have landed. Or more accurately, when. But my eyelids are so heavy. Why can't I open my eyes?

Don't panic. One thought at a time. Back to breathing. In, out. In, out. In, out…. keep it steady. Jesus, how hard is it to do the simplest thing?

Beep….. Beep….. Beep…..

"What's the story on this one? Any ID?" the doctor was asking as I groggily tried to clear the cobwebs from my brain. My grasp on consciousness appears to be pretty weak today.

"Nothing confirmed, Dr. Kelvin. The paramedics claim she must have been involved in a hit-and-run. She's in pretty bad shape for a simple accident, though." Rustling around my bed detailed the nurse's movements as she checked the equipment. "And it's strange. They said she just appeared on the road in front of them. He's blaming it on the weather, that they couldn't see her, but there's no impact damage to the ambulance. She's lucky to be alive."

Luck had nothing to do with it. Magick maybe, but luck I seem to be running light on at the moment. If it was luck, I never would have touched that cursed book and I sure wouldn't be wherever, or whenever, I am now.

Beep….. Beep….. Beep…..

"Nurse, how is she?" Pages flipped as Dr. Kelvin checked my chart, the noise dragging me back from the oblivion of sleep.

"She appears to be stabilizing. With all her injuries, I'm surprised she's not in a coma." Ms. Kennedy fussed with my blankets as the doctor reviewed the reports.

All what injuries? Give me the lowdown. What's broken? What's bruised? And what's clanging around in my head?? And can someone please turn down the volume on that thing!

I would really like to open my eyes now. And I am so thirsty! How about some water over here? A shot of whisky, maybe? Anything??

"Blood work is clear. Let's get her on a course of antibiotics. Except for her ribs, most of the injuries seem to be minor. Monitor any pain response and administer accordingly."

"Yes, Doctor."

Oh, NO! NO! NO! NO! Scan the fucking chip people! Please tell me I didn't fry the microchip…

As I fade out again, I wonder if maybe in this timeline I will be in a body that is not reactive to medication. What do you think the odds are? Since I have been universally screwed in many ways, I am not holding out hope that this little issue has been fixed…

This is not going to end well…

Beep….. Beep… Beep… Beep..Beep. Beep Beep.Beeeeeeeeeeep……

"She's crashing again!"

Didn't we just do this? What's with you people?

"Clear!"

Oh, shit! Not ag…. — SNAP — Christ! That is really fucking annoying.

Beep….. Beep….. Beep…..

My eyes flew open. At least they wanted to. A stickiness like glue coats my lashes. What the hell? As awareness of my physical body improves, I can sense the heaviness in my limbs, the limitations as I try to move anything. I could feel the energies of the nursing staff and the doctors, the machinery surrounding me. Well, those senses are working, even if I can't see yet. It helps to have a strong auric field to rely on. Thank God for small miracles. I'll take all of those He has to give.

Everything is fuzzy, like being wrapped in cotton batting. Just like my throat, come to think of it. Maybe if I just swallow… Concentrate… Damn, there's something in the way. Don't panic! Think first. If I set off those monitors, they'll be back in here, zapping me again. Okay, Stephanie, what do you remember? Well, apparently my name is Stephanie, if anyone is asking. What else? Right — modern hospital, crash cart, can't swallow… I AM in bad shape. Tubes in my throat. One mystery solved. Why am I breathing so deeply? What?!? I'm not breathing on my own! Shit!! I can't even control that!

Beep….. Beep… Beep… Beep.. Beep.. Beep..

Oops. Calm down. Let's not crash again. Slow and easy. Take a deep breath. — Very funny. I don't think I have a choice! Focus. Back to my inventory. Swallowing — not happening. Eyes open — a little bit…. come on!! Just a little more — nope. Not this time.

I am so tired…

Beep….. Beep….. Beep…..

You know, I could probably sleep better if that INCESSANT BEEPING WOULD STOP!

'Can you hear me? Honey?'

I got knocked out, didn't I. That voice, it's in my head, not in my ears. It's familiar, it's so warm, so gentle, so soothing… I smile as the image of Jack forms in my mind. I have been hearing his baritone for decades; it strums my heartstrings and fits into all the places in my soul that need filling.

'Hello, dear. Nice of you to find me, somehow. This telepathy thing is certainly enjoyable. I am think/talking to you, right? I'm not hallucinating….'

'I'm almost there. Hang on.' Jack's thoughts were twinged with worry and I could sense his eagerness to be with me.

'Not much choice there. I think I'm going to survive, but I am definitely stuck here, wherever here is… I really don't like hospitals. And I can't tell them about my challenges with medicine, so things

are a little dicey.'

'Haven't they scanned the chip!?'

'I don't think so... wait. Something's happening.... I don't feel so good....'

'SHIT! Why do you even have that thing!?'

Beep.Beep.Beep.Beeeeeeeeeep.....

"Doctor!"

Not again. I'm going to be fried from the inside out if this keeps up....

— SNAP — God DAMN it!!!

"What are you people doing?" cried Jack, as he rips the IV from my arm. "Are you TRYING to give her a heart attack?!"

"Sir, we just prevented one," the nurse said. "How did you get in here? This is a restricted area!"

"Prevented one! You made her crash by giving her those drugs! Didn't you even scan her microchip?" Jack's voice filled the room.

"Microchip?" Dr. Kennedy's voice interjected. "Sir, who are you? And what exactly is a microchip?"

Damn. Modern world, wrong timeline.

Chasing Ghosts

Time is not as linear as we are led to believe. In the past few years, I have travelled backwards, forwards, and sideways, dropping into times and places I could not envision as a young girl. I call the experience leaping or time-jumping, although neither succinctly describes what happens. Physically, I am always me, only somewhere, and somewhen, and once in a while, in my original time line.

This one appears to be a parallel one, almost the same, but not. Unfortunately, some things will never change. Apparently, I still react badly to medication, potentially fatally. This is a serious problem in any battle. If my enemies ever discover this, I can guarantee they will exploit my weakness. I mean, every heroine needs their Kryptonite. And a partner. Having a partner you trust with your life is an asset. No matter where I end up, he finds me, usually because he has to save me, often from my own ineptitude.

Jack is my hero, adaptable, street smart, and quick. There is an inner strength that he allows me to lean on, and he is definitely protective. Our telepathic link shares emotion as well as thoughts, and his words hum with energy. Now that my mind is clear, I can actually make real sentences and understand the answers. Speaking inside someone's head can be so invasive that we rarely use it. There are so many other skills in our arsenal. Today, separated, blind, and potentially in danger, I may need to rely on it for survival. Guess I should have paid closer attention to my training. Typical me—dash in, dash out, fly by the seat of my pants—wait, I am wearing pants, right? God, I am so messed up.

'Steph?'

'Mmmm.... yup, still feels like warm honey in my brain....'

'Stephanie!'

'You heard that?!? Damn it! Get out! No, wait. Don't go. I'm just weirded out. Are you two done sorting out who's in charge around here? And do I have to listen to that damn beeping all night?'

'First, it's the middle of the afternoon. Second, the doctor is in charge, but I told him you cannot be medicated. He's not the believing type. And since they have no experience with microchips, he's not the trusting type either. I guess the concept is a little strange to understand if the technology isn't on a similar path in this timeline.'

'Perhaps I should tattoo the information somewhere obvious. Assuming the language could be read, maybe I won't be fried while I am unconscious. And how did it get to be the afternoon? How long have I been time-slipping?'

'According to my TC, it's Tuesday the 14th of March —.'

'*What! It was the 5th last time I checked.*'

'*....in the year 4781.*'

'*Okay. Time to re-calibrate that gadget. Even in my condition, I know we can't hop centuries without seeing some improvements.*'

'*Oh, my scanner says it is 1981, but your chart says 4781.*'

'*I think my brain is melting. Must be all the kick-starts. Try again.*'

'*I read your medical chart. Twice. March 14, 4781.*'

'*Well, the easiest answer to all of this is that I am dreaming. Yup, that's it. I am floating somewhere in a dream, and when I wake up, my partner will make more sense. Let's try this again. Darling, what day is it?*' I sent sarcasm along with my thought to emphasize my displeasure.

'*Still March 14, 4781.*'

'*So if I clear some fog out of the way, you are telling me we went back a few decades, and ahead at the same time. Maybe I'll try some drugs after all.*'

'*I'm going to look for a research centre and figure out the 'whats' and 'wheres'. You good for a bit?*'

'*Where am I going to go?*' More sarcasm. My second favourite language.

With Jack wandering around… wherever we are, I returned to my more immediate quandary. I just need to remember what I was thinking about. Oh, right. Trying to make some sense of how I ended up somewhere in time, and probably, some time in space. The year we are in still baffles me. How did we arrive in 4781? Don't make myself crazier. I can't solve that mystery from here. Time for things I can do in my current state of being.

So, what do I know? I am in one piece, more or less. Now that the electricity is down to a dull roar, I should conduct a little physical assessment of my own. It would help if the beeping was lower too, but I guess I can't have everything.

Wait a minute. I am a witch, damn it. Turn the volume down. How hard can it be? Now, where is that infernal machine? Bats use echolocation. I should be able to do the same. Follow the beeps back to where they start… There! Found you. Now to push the buttons. No! Hold up. Bad idea. Mess with the wrong one and I am back under the paddles again. What if I unplug the unit altogether? That's another awful idea. How on Earth would they explain it? Man, I am so tired. Energy work was never this hard before. I must be in some seriously messed-up shape.

Beep….. Beep….. Beep…..

A hush has settled over the hospital. Nighttime. How many hours did I lose? Being blind leaves me at a disadvantage and being this vulnerable is making me very nervous. The beginning tendrils of anxiety curl like snakes in my stomach.

Beep… Beep… Beep… Beep…

Breathe. Breathe. Breathe. Relax. Panic won't help me. Even if the Ferin could follow our trail, it will take time to find out the 'where' in the 'when'. Without identification, my existence in the timeline may remain a mystery for a while.

My nap has made me feel more alive. And thirsty. I am so fucking thirsty. There is a grittiness in my throat like I swallowed half the desert and then left some behind. Can't we remove this tube? Maybe I can crush it a bit, shrink it down so I can work around it. That shouldn't be too obvious, right? Plus, I have nothing better to do, anyway.

"How is the patient doing?" The words ooze into the room, announcing a visitor.

Shit. No tube shrinking for the moment. But who is this now? The voice is familiar, but not from the past few hours. And it's too quiet… Why did the beeping stop?

"You hid yourself well this time. But I can tell you aren't in any shape to slip away from us." Her energy is oppressive and heavy as she leans over my bed. "We want the Book, witch. I know you can hear me. Your heartbeat still shows on the monitor, even though I turned off the alert sensor." The soft brushing of fabric as she moves around the room helps me to pinpoint her location. "This is pretty primitive, considering. But it works. And I can sense you panicking. Maybe I should pull the plug. They could come shock you again. That would be fun to watch after all the damage you have caused."

She's right. I am panicking. They found me already. And Jack. Where's Jack! Damn it, man. I'm in real trouble now!

Footsteps on the tile floor announce a new arrival. "Pardon me, miss. Can I see some identification, please?"

Let her go! Just let her go! I don't want anyone to die today! Please, let her go….

"Can I get security in here?!"

Shit, here it comes…

"I'm sorry, nurse. This must be the wrong room. I was looking for a friend of mine, but this patient is not my friend."

You've got that right, sister. I did not understand how much attention I would bring to myself when I picked up that dusty old book. How was I supposed to know so many people wanted it, especially after all those centuries? Damn thing should've stayed lost.

'Stephanie, is everything OK?'

'Jack!' Oh, Jack, they found me. One of them is here, in the hospital. She was just in my room!'

The twin energies moved away from the bedside. My head shifted, and I focused on what I could hear, trying to locate where they had gone.

'Shit! I'm on my way up. Hold tight!'

Again with the humour. My strength is returning, but I am not going anywhere fast without my sight.

Beep….. Beep….. Beep…..

I never thought I would be happy to hear that fucking noise. I need to get my wits about me and I must stay conscious. Where there is one member of the Council, the rest of the team won't be far behind. Time to pull it together, Stephanie DuMonde, or this will be one short-lived leap and I didn't survive being jump-started just to cash it in to some anti-knight.

"Let's check these bandages. See how you are doing." Ms. Kennedy has returned.

Yes, let's. Give me all the news, sweetheart. How bad is it? With the tube in the way, the nurse can't hear me, but my intent must have translated.

"Well, things don't look as bad as everyone says. Why don't you try opening your eyes? I know you can hear me, miss. Your eyes are darting under the lids. Come on now. Harder."

It is brighter in the room, light making its way around my eyelids, seeping in through my lashes. Maybe I'm not truly blind. Maybe I had just been so swaddled up I couldn't open my eyes. Please, God, let the light in… As I slowly, oh so slowly, make my lids move, I realize this is taking more energy than I have to spare. Help me, God. Goddess. Anybody. Give me a bit more strength.

Nothing.

Where is everybody? I am so tired....

Beep….. Beep….. Beep…..

'Steph.'

'Steph.'

"Stephanie. Wake up."

"Just five more minutes, mom...."

"Ha. Ha. Very funny. Come on, Sleeping Beauty. Time to rise and shine, or at least to open your eyes."

"Excuse me, sir. We would like to take care of our patient now." The nurse has returned and appears to be on a mission.

"Of course. I'll wait out in the hallway." Jack gripped my hand before letting it drop back onto the bed.

"So, your name is Stephanie. That is more than we had yesterday. Let's add it to your chart and take a look at you." The nurse started her routine checks. "If you can hear me, I want you to nod your head. Can you do that for me?"

Obliging the hospital staff seemed innocent enough. The monitor kept rhythm with my motion as I moved my head up and down, seeming alternately louder and quieter as I played with which way I could tune in more clearly. My sense of hearing was working overtime as I listened to the pages of my chart being turned and the rustle of the nurse's uniform when she approached my bed.

"Looks like you are ready to lose that tube. Let's get a team in here and clear your airway, okay?"

I would have kissed her if I were mobile. Removing the tube was welcome news. Now to stay awake long enough for the team to do their job. The rattle of wobbly cart wheels and multiple footsteps marked the arrival of more staff.

Fifteen long minutes later, a much-needed sip of water wound its way past the scrapes and scratches. The medical staff seemed pleased with my progress. From the doorway, the doctor commented on how quickly I was improving. Staying any longer was not an option.

"So, you're off that machine, I see. Ready to get back to work?" Jack had reentered the room after the last nurse cleared out.

Who invited the drill sergeant to the party? Sigh….. My eyes peeled open, the sensation of taffy pulling apart, adding to my distress.

"I'm not seeing anything!" My voice contained more than a bit of anxiety as my hands flew to my face. Nothing held my eyes closed, no external impairment to my vision. But inside, all was black.

"Whoa! What happened to your eyes?"

"Thanks for adding to my panic. What is wrong with my eyes?!"

Beep..Beep..Beep..Beep…

"They appear normal… except for the strange glow."

Time for a genuine panic attack. Pull yourself together, Stephanie DuMonde. Breathe. Breathe. Oh, it is so wonderful to do that on my own again.

"So, I'm blind then. Perfect. I have a team of assassins on my ass and I can't see them coming. But I glow in the dark! Could this day get any worse?!" I can hear the sarcasm in my voice, a defence mechanism this time, something to keep the fear at a distance.

Phwap!Phwap!Phwap!Phwap!Phwap!

Beep.Beep.Beep.Beep.Beep.Beep…

"Move! Move! Move!"

That wasn't me or Jack. I am going out on a limb here and assume my visitors told two friends, who told two friends, who decided to turn this hospital wing into a party zone.

Perfect. Just what we needed.

'Honey? Is that gunfire?' I definitely overuse sarcasm with my inside voice. *'How close are they this time?'*

Nothing.

"Oh, Jack?!?" My voice sounds like I am drawing sandpaper across tightly drawn violin strings and carries the raspiness of a three-pack-a-day smoker.

"I'm here, love. Just working out a way to move you."

"Is that even an option? What are our chances of protecting ourselves right here?" In the meantime, my fingers travelled along my arms, searching for the wires and tubes they have me hooked up to. I can't take the equipment with me.

"Shhh….."

Right. Think it, don't say it. No better time to practice this telepathy thing.

'What weapons do we have? How can I help?' Removing the last of the leads, I sat up fully and swung my legs out of the bed. The swimming sensation lingered before my body adjusted to being vertical. Just because I heal more rapidly than most, unfortunately, doesn't mean I'm going to be at full strength in the next five minutes.

'Ummmm....'

'You know I can "hear" you... I am blind, not helpless. We've worked blind before. I'm just rusty.'

Jack paused before responding. 'Take my hand, Steph. I can guide you, just for now.'

Boy, does he know me, or what? On any other day, there is no way I would take help, not from him, not from anybody. But considering the present circumstances…. Allowing myself a fragment of time to ground, orient, and focus, I dropped the barriers keeping the energies at bay and let the torrent of emotions wash over me. A hospital is not a wonderful place to be energetically wide open. It will take much of my energy to move and stay alive. Everybody else will need to wait for their turn. Time to seek some outside help.

Expanding my aura to access those of the rooms and hallways around us, I sensed the souls of people who have passed over, those about to, and those fighting to hang on to a life that is no longer theirs. One light shines more brightly, and I focus on it.

'Go left. We have a guide there.'

'Are you sure? We only have one shot at this.'

Doubt nibbles at my brain, but the light continues to beckon to me.

'Cover my eyes, please. Grab anything you can. I don't want them acting as a beacon. The Ferin are capable enough without giving *them an easy target.'*

Keeping my eyes closed as he wrapped my head with gauze, I used the precious seconds to make a stronger connection to the soul of the young girl standing in the hallway. She had been no more than twelve, yet so worldly in her gaze. No child should be witness to such destruction.

PHWAP! PHWAP! PHWAP!

'They're a little close for comfort, Steph. Time to move. Can you run?'

'We're about to find out. If something pops up, think the directions to me before you turn.' I stepped close to Jack's back and placed my left hand on his shoulder. Everything in me is screaming that being in the rear is the worst place to be in this firefight. My hindered presence will be a concern, as I cannot see any enemies approaching from behind. Well, every day should include a fresh challenge. Next time, Universe, send one at a time.

Deciding it will not help to think about where the death squads are, I leave our defensive strategy to my partner. I focus on the spirit child, guiding us to her, hoping the entire time that she intends to get us out of harm's way, not into it. My legs, while still shaky, seemed willing enough to support my weight. I sent a silent prayer to find a safe place and avoid the enemy agents. It was all fine to talk tough, but I was a liability at the moment, using most of my energy just to stay upright.

'When the path is clear, head down the hall to the right. She's about six doors down.'

'Got it. Going right. Now.'

And so began our desperate scramble to remain among the living. I tried to tune out the surrounding sounds, but without my sight, every other sense is heightened. My hearing reached an almost painful frequency, with every machine, every voice, step, scream and cry blending into a rock concert level hum. Below the surface ran the emotional slurry of grief and panic, loss and dying. Add in the smell of fear so strong it even beats out the odour of death. There is so much death here…

Shake it off, Steph. Get a grip. Focus. Ground. Breathe. In. Out. In. Out. In. Out.

While I was having my moment, we continued making our way down the hallway, trying to stay hidden, but we could be out in the open at any second.

'To the right, Jack. She's turned into a small corridor.'

'Looking.'

'Now. Right now.'

'There's no corridor. Only a blank wall.'

Shit.

Overload

Following ghosts can be tricky. They forget living folk can't walk through walls.

'There has to be a door. She is waiting just beyond this wall, calling us in. Maybe on the other side of one of these rooms?'

Time for a more one-on-one connection. I hate interfering with the dead. They should be able to go about their own business. But I need more information, or we will soon join her in the no-longer mortal realm.

Jack released my grip to search for a way into the adjacent rooms while I reached out to the child and ask her for a little more help. Without warning, Jack grabbed my hand and pulled me inside a tiny room, not much more than a closet.

'Picked a lock, did you? Where are we?' I asked.

'Looks like an abandoned storage room. There's a door in the back. For a second I could see light under it, but I don't know where it goes.'

As I scan for the spirit we had followed, I pick up the approach of several less-than-human energies.

'We've run out of options. Get us in there!'

Jack pushed me through into the deeper black of the hidden room. In the rush to block the door behind us, he dropped my hand, leaving me completely alone with my thoughts — and they were not pleasant ones. How did they get so many Ferin into this time stream, and so quickly? They are getting serious about this retrieval, and I don't think they mean to bring us in alive.

"Jack?" I whispered, my voice sounding loud despite the minimal volume.

'Jack??'

'Right here.' Jack took my hand, though I now knew where he was. The strange light in my eyes was providing outlines I couldn't distinguish before. Even through the gauze, with my eyes closed as tightly as possible, my sight was returning, in a fashion. The images remind me of night vision goggles, though I'm not sure how helpful distinguishing aura fields in the dark will be. If I only had time to test it out, to experiment with what I can really 'see'. But no. Like everything else lately, I will have to learn on the fly, trust my intuition, and hope I guess right.

"Team 3 to Team 4. 9th floor secure. No sighting. Over."

"Team 4 to Team 3. Proceed to the 10th floor. Leave no witnesses. Over."

"Roger that."

The sound of footsteps outside the storage room door made my pulse race. I clenched my eyes shut, covering them with my clothes, praying no sliver of light would be visible to give us away. Jack, ever ready for danger, gave my hand a touch before sliding away in the darkness to take up a better defensive position.

PHWAP! PHWAP! PHWAP!

My heart aches for these poor people who had done nothing wrong today. They got up, ate breakfast, said goodbye to their families, and came to work. Life should have gone on for them, been routine. And then we came along. How many more lives have been sacrificed for a book so old we struggle to find any records of it in all the archives known to man? How can I ignore the slaughter going on just beyond my hiding place? The grief is overwhelming, and a sob collects in my throat. Holding myself together, I release the pain and anguish, the guilt I feel that this mess is all my fault. The guilt I am going to have to accept, for I did take the Book. And the more the Ferin try to get it back, the more confident I am that I needed to do exactly that.

But the knowledge does not make my heart hurt any less.

Phwap! Phwap! Phwap!

The gunfire moves away from our hideout, allowing my shoulders to relax. I can feel the tension leaving Jack, pooling at our feet, and slowly melting into the floor. As he takes my hand, my whole being crumbles and silently cries for all the loss we have been witness to today, for all the suffering our presence has caused. Jack holds me close and I follow the tracks of his warm tears as they fall onto my neck, for he is nearly as human as I am, as grief-stricken at the massacre the Ferin are so callously perpetrating. They well know how this devastation tears at our very souls. These people mean nothing more to them than a means of making us suffer, to have us capitulate to save those that are still alive. This is the unfairness of the war we have found ourselves in. We have become complicit in the deaths of so many in order to protect the rest of the Universe.

Through my grief came the alarms and sirens, the sounds of the living trying to help those that can yet be saved. I sent out a wish that some make it home tonight when hundreds will not. But we are not yet out of this, and now I know how difficult our escape will be. Nine floors of Council assassins, sweeping the building repeatedly, looking for us and the book. I am certain they are not above using non-ethical practices to extort the information from us about where we have secreted the precious tome. Being captured is not an option.

"Alpha Team Leader to Base. Alpha Team Leader to Base."

"Go Alpha Team Leader."

"9th floor is secure. Repeat. 9th floor is secure."

"Copy. Proceed to 10. Over."

"Copy that. Proceeding to 10. Out."

Well, there is a surprise. This timeline has a very responsive military, maybe SWAT. Whoever they are, as long as they are not alien life forms, I welcome them. I wonder what they will make of the not-so-human bloodstains they will encounter as they clear out the Ferin. Having gone a few rounds with these creatures, they may look human, but they certainly don't bleed out the same.

'Should we move, Jack? Do you think it is safe?'

Jack continued to listen to the movements in the hallway. While he is concentrating on the success, or failure, of the rescue teams, I realize I have given no further thought to the ghost who led us to this refuge. Without lifting my head, I extend my aura to sense where she is. Only an empty space filled with peace and calm remains. The simple act of kindness released her soul from this plain, and she has continued on her journey. With regret that I had not thanked her, I send a message of love along the path behind her, praying it will reach the child when she needs it most.

Saturated energy flows around us from the dead, the dying, the wounded, blending with the hope and dedication of those working so hard to save so few. Without walking among them, I still marvel at their ability to push emotions aside, to focus and perform miracles of medicine to have just one win to pull them onto the next. But we need to leave this area, hide within the survivors and hope the Ferin have been driven off, or (dare I dream) killed. I would wish for capture in any other situation, but an imprisoned Council assassin is far more dangerous than a dead one. They appear to have a built-in tracking system to find their injured or missing brothers, much like ants do to bring their comrades back to the nest.

Jack moved to the outer room to assess what materials are at our disposal. With little more than a few chemicals and a ball of string, Jack could blow up half of this building, but we are not looking for any more demolition or destruction. A nice set of greens would do nicely. Maybe a wheelchair, because I am suddenly not feeling so well.....

A Little Breather

Beep….. Beep….. Beep…..

This was all a dream, right? I am waking up from a brief nap and —

Shit. The gauze over my eyes says otherwise. This sucks. On the plus side, I am obviously still alive, but so many are not. Before I can sink any further into that thought, a shift in the energy tells me Jack has arrived. Overwhelmed by a rush of relief, I reach for his hand. His skin, so rough and sturdy, gives me strength and helps me regain my sense of balance.

"How bad is it? I guess I fainted. Big tough witch." My attempt to lighten the mood was feeble, but I had to say something. Okay, it was more like a squawk, but I managed it without peeling the remaining skin out of my throat.

"I helped where I could after I got you back into your room. There is —-. Let's talk about it later. We need to get your strength back 'cause I don't think they're done searching for us yet." To distract himself, Jack set about untangling the cotton swaddling my head.

Knowing Jack as well as I do, there is much he has walled off from me. Some is for my own good, but much is also for his. Being unconscious saved me from the horrors he must have seen, the torment he must have felt. It would not assuage the guilt of surviving. We were one of their 'miracles', but it feels hollow. Tears slide down my cheeks. Jack gently wipes them away and kisses me on each eye, the slightest feather of a touch. Something inside me shifts and moves, responding to the magic between us, and I know, rather than sense, that the light in my eyes has dimmed.

When your Universal guides take control of your life, things happen for reasons that make absolutely no sense until after the fact. My apparent blindness and affliction assisted us when we needed to 'see' in the dark. My injuries also kept us from participating in a fight we would have surely lost. And my unconscious state spared me from the horrors Jack bore witness to. I would never wish such trauma on him. The Universe knows he is so much better at separating himself from the situation than I am, more capable of segmenting the visual impact into acceptable stimuli than I ever could. Does that make me a weak partner? Sometimes I think I should be stronger, but even after all of our battles, I am not immune to the effects. And Jack needs my moments of weakness, for they make his strengths more apparent. Besides, I can always kick his ass in the ring if I ever need a reality check.

It feels good to blink. Gradually, my vision returns and the hyper-focus of my other senses dies down. While Jack plots our escape, I slowly sip my apple juice and debate eating the green jello sitting on the tray beside my bed. Fatigue grabs me and I drift in and out of consciousness. I am not as strong as I believe. The indistinct noises of the hospital fade as I fall into a well of memories, fragments of a life long passed.

Snippets of thoughts. Questions unanswered. I have lived in defiance of all they taught me as a child. The church and its congregation supported the poor, such as we were. Mother attended service, listened as the children said prayers before bed. Father gave every tithe even as little as we had. Ironic. And in the end, the only one of our family to be spared is the one who never truly believed in the existence of God.

That much of my childhood, I do remember. I remember questioning how one being could control everything for so long. Through it all, I still believe in Heaven. I live with the eternal hope my family made it there peacefully after their traumatic passing in the icy waters of the Atlantic. My siblings should have lived long and fruitful lives in the new world we planned on reaching. Instead, in a way, I am living their years for them. When the waves carried me to shore in 1873, I was sixteen years old, going on sixty. I lost all that I knew — my homeland, my family, my reason for living. So much has changed in the following century, plus some. I often meet such reflections with a sigh of perceived fatigue that comes with an extended life.

Tucked deep in my heart, I hold faded images of my family, their vibrancy decaying over time. What I recall most vividly is the cold. It was so very cold. And dark. I would never believe any place could be so unforgiving, but the Atlantic ocean has no feelings, couldn't care less who drowns within her waves. I suppose I was one of the lucky ones that night—or maybe luck had nothing to do with that night, either.

Down and Out

"Stephanie, are you listening to me?"

"What? Oh, sorry. I was daydreaming. Did you work out a plan?" I'm certain he has. I am merely being polite, seeing as I had been ignoring him.

"I'm going to find us some scrubs from the lounge down the hall. Wait for me to get back. Stretch or something. You seem a little stiff."

A little stiff? I was hit by a bus, or perhaps a tank, and left for dead. Grumbling about what a drill sergeant he is, I gingerly did as he suggested. Decades of martial arts training have given me a supple body, but it needs constant work to keep it in shape. Muscle memory only goes so far, and if the Ferin are close, I needed to remind my muscles how to behave. I worked through a simple set of stretches, slowly moving into rudimentary yoga, letting my idle mind reach out to sense the activity on the floor surrounding us. While the tension created by the attack lessened and the noise level diminished, the emotional keening grew with each dead body located amongst the wreckage. This scene will live in the memories of the survivors for a long time. I am once again grateful I could not see the carnage and will do all I can to isolate myself from it as we make our way out of this battleground.

"Oh good. You made it. I was so worried." Sarcasm drips off her every word. The scout is back.

"How kind of you to check up on me. I was worried you might have been killed with all the rest." I can do sarcasm too. *Jack! Get back here fast!'* Telepathy must be good for something, like saving my ass again.

"They're not all dead, sweetheart. Just re-grouping. These humans were faster to respond than expected. We'll know better the next time."

"What makes you think there will be a next time? I don't plan to be here waiting for them, and obviously, you aren't up to the task." Probably not an outstanding idea to provoke her, but I tend to gamble with my life if I think Jack will come to the rescue.

"Honey, I would hate to break a nail punching you in the face for that remark. But it might be worth it to knock some of that smugness back down your throat!"

Subtly, I moved into a more defensive posture. My eyesight is still hazy, but a scan of her aura proves useful. The scout is sending out subtle waves of yellow and red. She thinks she can take me. Let's see her try. A grim smile crossed my lips as I prepared to beat the sassiness right out of her.

I'd like to be able to tell you what happened next, but in all honesty, I have no idea. She simply 'winked out', like someone turned off her switch. Even when someone dies, it takes time for their aura to detach and drift away. This was so instantaneous I stood with my mouth open, totally stunned. With my blurred vision, I struggled to see if her body lay on the floor. Leaving a Ferin behind would have an entire timeline trying to figure out where aliens come from. As if they haven't left enough clues strewn about today. Approaching the spot where I had sensed her last, nothing remained. Not even a smear on the tiles. What the heck??

Jack raced into the room, finally responding to my telepathic 911. Slamming to a halt, he looked around for the threat, to which I sheepishly shrugged my shoulders and held my hand out for a set of scrubs. Having already taken a minute to change in the lounge where he had found the clothing, Jack looked like he belonged here. Time for me to do the same.

"So, where'd she go?"

"Wonderful question. I have never seen someone vanish in an instant before. There's no sign she was here at all."

Jack paused for a moment, thinking at his usual lightning speed. "You don't suppose the scouts are holographic, do you?"

To be honest, the thought had not crossed my mind. Her disappearing act had unnerved me and I had not taken it to the next logical level yet. Trust Jack to process it faster. He packed our clothes into a backpack and slung it over his shoulder. Inspecting the room, not wanting to leave any trace behind, Jack pulled my bag out of the closet and put the strap in my hand.

"It would explain how they can follow us so precisely without suffering the side effects of the time jumps. But how are they locking on to us, to begin with?" I replied.

"That's a puzzle for a quieter moment. Right now, we need to move. The SWAT team is sweeping through the hospital again, and I don't want to be here for the question-and-answer period of today's events."

Jack reached for my other hand, and I let him take it. Time enough for liberalism when we are safely away from here. After scanning the hallway for Ferin and the military teams, we made our way through the mass of confused and scared people. Keeping to the edges, we let gurneys carrying the wounded pass by, our heads down to minimize being described later, and gradually reached the stairwell. Any departure route is risky. Elevators are closed spaces with limited exit points, definitely a great place to trap your quarry. Stairwells are therefore the preferred egress of any escapee. But the pursuing force follows the same playbook. This is a game of timing, more than it is of skill. Do we make them think we took the stairs but really hopped into the elevator? Do we go up, then down? Or do we roll the dice on them trying to out-think us and stick with the simplest path?

The convoluted path won, and we ended up walking it, mainly

because we were out of options. Trusting our pursuers would have the identical problem, we continued weaving our way through the hallways, sometimes finding stairs going down, sometimes going back up on another flight. If I had to retrace our steps, I would have needed at least one ball of string and a guide to do it. And the whole time, the sounds and smells of the event pressed in on us. It took the bulk of my strength to walk, so my boundaries were buckling under the energetic pressure.

Sensing my flagging resolve, Jack found a wheelchair and pushed me into it, against my protests. There was no easy way to navigate through all the damaged areas. Three minutes was all I had to shore up my defences, but it was a good start. Risking an overload of empathic waves, I opened the channels to search for any threat to us, in particular the scout whose signature I now knew by heart. For a singular moment, I sensed a glow on the floor above us, but it faded as we heard the echoes of gunfire. The Ferin were rousted, but the locals would not protect us if they discovered we caused the invasion. Experts and specialists would pour over the building for days, looking for survivors, collecting samples and making charts. I hoped they had logged nothing more about my blood than its type.

Leaving the wheelchair for someone who needed it more than I did, we made our way to the elevator and joined the crowd of quietly crying people. Shell-shocked looks and anger seeped from them as they all patiently waited for their turn. It seemed so normal I almost cried myself. I sensed the officers before they rounded the corner. Jack grabbed my hand in case we needed to run, but they weren't searching for two hospital employees. Breathing as regularly as possible, we nodded our thanks to them as they moved on.

Stepping in with as many people as could fit, we jostled and settled ourselves, becoming separated. Mild panic flew through me as we parted. I had not realized my reliance on Jack until that moment.

'Don't look at me, Steph. Just breathe. You know I am still here. I won't leave without you. Let everyone else step off first. Reach your right hand towards me, so I can grab it.'

Relief. Why do I put so much stock in being tough and strong? Today, if only for this moment, I will let weakness be my guide. It's possible this is another test, another lesson I need to learn. Looking back at my life, I rarely embrace weakness of any kind. It has proven to be a potentially fatal flaw in the past.

Upon reaching the main floor, the doors opened to more noise and chaos. As the group stepped off ahead of us, we heard the squawk of a radio: "…two patients unaccounted for from the 9th floor. Be on the lookout for one senior male, 5 foot 10, using a cane or walker, and one female, 30, brunette. May be travelling with a male companion, also 30, brown hair…."

WTF! Jack stepped back and rapidly pounded the buttons to take us to the basement and the parking levels. Why are we on their radar? Or perhaps I am paranoid. Maybe there is another 30-something chick wandering around here with a guy who may or may not have caused this entire calamity.

Jack quickly scanned the area as he pulled me from the elevator and along the wall. Cautiously, we moved through the tidy rows of abandoned cars and the bodies strewn throughout the cavernous parking level. The added stress was showing. Feeling sluggish, I slowed down, not able to catch all the information he was sharing with me, either mentally or physically. It was all I could do to keep up. My energy faltered. Cold metal tugged at my skin as I slid down the fender of the nearest car. Scooping me up, he dumped me into the back seat. No stranger to hot-wiring a car, Jack pulled the wiring harness down and sparked the engine to life while I settled in, making myself small, conserving my strength.

We are not out of the woods yet. The path is littered with bits and pieces discarded during the panic, not to mention lives lost on this level. The Ferin had decimated this building. We cautiously drove through the darkened structure, navigating around obstacles and debris as carefully as we could. Had I been stronger, we would have made faster progress by walking. Jack stopped to get out and move a pair of bodies, carefully laying them off to the side. My heart broke for him.

Through the glass, I watched the souls of the dead. They were just hanging around as if they didn't know there was a better place to be now that they were free of their physical frames. The couple before us seemed lost. Near every corpse, there was a soul, just lingering. There were so many. I wondered why I was seeing more down here when I didn't remember there being as many in the upper levels. Maybe I needed to be in a less heightened state. Lord knows I wasn't relaxing much today. In fact, I had done nothing well today. It wasn't just my fatigue; my stomach was throwing in its opinion.

"I don't suppose you packed a sandwich or something."

"Not the best time, Steph."

"I should have eaten the jello."

"Seriously. You are hungry right now."

"When am I not hungry?"

Jack sighed and kept his eyes on our path. I turned to watch out the rear window. Jack always has my back. For now, maybe I could have his.

Meeting Jack

I haven't always been the best partner for him. When we first met, I may have attempted to take his head off.

Being chased out of town after town, fending for myself any way I could, I had become fairly proficient with my personal protection and at spotting danger from a distance. And Jack smelled like all kinds of danger.

Sometimes a girl just has to have company, if you know what I mean, so when I stumbled into a new town one dreary afternoon, the local watering hole seemed like a suitable place to sit and figure out where I had landed. Ed's Tavern, established in 1867. Not a bad run in those days, assuming Ed was still alive thirty years later.

Tying my horse to the rail, I looked around the small town. Seeing no one out on the street, the lack of activity in the middle of the day puzzled me. As I opened the doors to the tavern, all heads turned. I am used to the look, always being the new girl in town. It was the open hostility that took me by surprise. Not the friendly greeting one would normally find, and as hands reached for their sidearms, I smoothly moved to the bar to order a drink, anxious to defuse the situation before someone, namely me, got shot.

"What's the house special, barkeep?"

"We don't serve your kind around here," the bartender sneered with a mocking tone, as he dragged his eyes down and up my body.

I raised one eyebrow and coldly asked, "What kind would that be, sir?"

As if by one thought, I heard the revolvers clear their holsters with a barely audible snap of leather. Deciding I had nothing to lose, I moved with visible deliberation, reaching for the purse tucked between the folds of my riding gear, and pulled out a tiny bit of coin. It was enough to buy my drink and a few more, but not enough to be flashy.

"Your money's no good here, catin," came a voice from behind me.

Without turning around, I coolly replied, "You assume wrongly, sir. I am travelling alone out of necessity, wanting nothing more than a cold drink."

"I said your money's no good. Now, I don't usually hit women, but since you look like you might like it, I'll give it a swing if you don't pack on out."

Not understanding what I had walked into, and not one to

back down from a challenge, especially one I can easily win, I turned and let the cowboy see that I, too, held a piece. A lot of things can hide inside clothing. Much of the time, I could outfit a small army with what I carried. But this day, I was limited since I had not been looking for a fight. Somehow, though, a fight appeared to be looking for me. Keeping one eye on the jackass who had consumed too much liquid courage, and one on the rest of the room, I resumed my conversation with the bartender.

"Are you sure my money is no good here? I only want one. The rest is yours."

He swallowed, counting the profit in his head, then slowly shook it. "No can do. This town doesn't want you here. You'd best get on your horse and be gone before sundown."

One: How does this town know who I am? Word travels in slow motion across a country as vast as this, unless there was a telegraph station here somewhere. I must be slipping if I missed that on the way in. And two, why so eager for me to leave before dark encroaches? His words sounded like more than a common saying, more of a true warning.

Pocketing my coin, I cautiously edged my way back to the door. Looking out at the street, I could see a man holding the reins to my stallion. Finding this very odd, I sidestepped out and looked around for additional threats, hidden enemies, the glint of a barrel in a window. Nothing. Still watching the tavern patrons, I approached my horse and took the bridle as the man dropped it, clearly afraid to let me touch him. As I swung into the saddle, I took a moment to make eye contact and test his energy field. Fear. All I found was fear. A fear so deep and pervasive, no amount of talking would make him believe I was not the enemy. But something was out there, and they were awaiting its arrival. What kind of a 'thing' could it be that they are drinking up half the bar stock to face it tonight?

Curiosity gets me in all kinds of trouble. I couldn't leave town without investigating the cause of their anxiety. The townsfolk made it hard to learn anything, though, when not one human soul around would look at me, let alone talk. All doors and windows were rapidly being shuttered and barred. The hotel had fifteen empty rooms, but none for me. Even the local bordello turned me away. Now that was insulting. How bad are things when you can't even buy a room in a brothel for the night?

Hungry and thirsty, I moved out of Deadman's Pass and made up camp at the edge of a small river running behind the houses. Leaving my horse to graze, I circled the town on foot, staying tucked in the gradually forming shadows, trying to figure out what the hell was going on. It occurred to me I would likely get shot if I kept it up, so when no solution to the mystery presented itself, I returned to my steed to wait for night to fall.

Now, if you have never done a stakeout before, let me tell you, there is nothing more boring to do on this planet or any other. Tying myself in my saddle, knowing the horse would alert me to danger, I drifted off into a light sleep. I am such an idiot. I don't know why I thought a nap would make me sharper in case of a fight, but being jerked awake by my stallion stampeding under me proved I was wrong. The ties held, but at a cost to my body. Whiplash and crushed ribs took the wind out of me, and brush pummelled me as the horse ran in a panic from whatever was behind us in the night. Painfully pulling myself down over the saddle, I protected my face and felt for a weapon to use in the fight I knew was coming. Allowing my psychic vision to help me, I sent out feelers to see what I was dealing with. Nothing. Nothing but blackness, emptiness. That's not possible. Everything has an energy signature, everything can be felt if you know how.

As the sensation of danger increased, my steed panicked and tried to jump to the opposite bank in a desperate attempt to escape. Seeing disaster ahead, I quickly loosened the reins and prepared to hit the icy water, praying I held onto my knife when it happened. The horse rolled onto its side as it impacted, and I was thrown into the churning river. I would have appreciated more water in that part of the riverbed, instead of the numerous rocks I came into contact with. Sputtering and spewing river water, I shook my head and crawled to the bank, grabbing any grasses and branches that would support me, hoping to reach solid ground before I was forced to protect myself.

Behind me, I heard the desperate squeals of my struggling horse. Self-preservation kept it moving until it regained its footing and climbed out on the other side. I hoped he would find a safe place to wait for me, assuming I survived.

"Well, well, well. What do we have here?"

That line is so cliché, but it's what he said. Scout's honour.

Cold, wet, hungry, and aching in more than a dozen places, I was not in the mood to banter with a stranger, and certainly not with one I could not see or sense. I resisted the urge to panic, straightened up, and wiped mud and hair from my eyes before facing the voice in the night. Shaking the water from my hands, I wrung out my clothing, pretending I wasn't petrified.

"Here you have a woman who has been thrown by her horse and nearly drowned in this fucking river, and all you can do is stand there and be funny. Didn't your mother raise you better than that?!"

Staring straight into the darkness, looking for some sign of what was there, I sensed the energy of the being gathering, like mist on a pane of glass sliding together to become a bead of water. The form of a man appeared as the mass continued to collect, the blackness darkening in one place, gradually taking shape in the moonlight filtering through the trees surrounding us.

"You do not want to get any closer to him," another voice carried out of the deepening gloom.

If I may be honest, I might have shit myself right then, had I eaten anything that day. My feet definitely left the ground, and I whirled around with my blade in motion, cleanly cutting the air where the newest apparition had, well, appeared. And that was how I met Jack.

Leaving Your Troubles Behind

P HWAP!PHWAP!PHWAP!PHWAP!PHWAP!

A barrage of bullets struck the rear of the car as we reached the last ramp of the parking structure. Shattered glass sprinkled the back seat. Luckily, I was crouching down, trying to be a smaller target. I need to stop daydreaming in the middle of a battle.

"Where the FUCK did they come from!?!" Jack sounded pissed, and I didn't blame him. His extra eyes, mainly mine, were not exactly earning their keep today. I poked my head up high enough to search for our attackers, but Jack had already exited the building and was swerving into traffic. We would be easy to spot with bullet holes in the trunk and a missing rear window. Since we knew nothing of the city and had no time for proper reconnaissance, this would be the epitome of "winging it".

"Does this remind you of anything?" I asked Jack, mostly to take my mind off of our predicament.

Jack chuckled. "Do you mean the day we escaped from the

mob in Chicago? Or the time we stole the painting out of the Louvre?"

"Actually, I was thinking about the run we made across the Sahara desert with the Legionnaires on our tail."

"Oh, yeah, that was a fun one." Jack continued driving, analyzing and searching for a suitable escape route.

By the time we get to the 'where', he will have figured out the 'how'. I took another chance to look for Council assassins or police cars. Blue and red flashing lights in the oncoming traffic showed the next shift of responders heading for the disaster we were determined to put behind us. Scanning the auras of every driver surrounding us would be draining, but I didn't see any other way to ensure we were not being followed by the Ferin.

Hopefully, my time daydreaming was enough to recharge my psychic batteries. I sent a pulse of energy to interact with anything on the road. The traffic should keep us hidden among the multitude of commuters. Most of the targets within range were simply people heading to their destinations, their focus on getting home or on the news reports flooding the airwaves. Thoughts were varied and while most showed concern, they had little to do with our current situation.

Until I reached out a little further.

Several cars back, I picked up the frantic energy of someone under the influence of a compulsion spell. The driver of a small suburban in the lane behind us was single-mindedly looking for a man and a woman in a gun-riddled sedan. Searching his mind for other thoughts or energies, his panic, frustration and confusion all slammed into my probe. His brain was not his own for the time being, and maybe never would be again. The Council and their mind-control spells are brutal. It tempted me to send a spell of forgetfulness back along the channel I was using, but any counter-spell would light us up in the darkness. I knew the man had but minutes to live, longer if he had anything to report. But Ferin scouts only use their puppets for a brief time before terminating them. I have not yet learned what makes them so callous, so quick to snuff out lives that, before them, had been wonderful ones. These productive and caring individuals made one move that changed everything: they appeared in the path of a Council member in need of information. It was that simple. Time to protect our position. I locked an energy tag on the Ferin's unwilling spy and turned my efforts to cloaking our own vehicle and diverting attention.

Since I had been nearing unconsciousness when Jack dropped me into the back seat of our sedan, I needed a better idea of what we were driving. Staying small and unrecognizable, I peered over the edge of the window to confirm the car's colour and determine what the rear panels looked like. In order to mask the bullet holes, I needed to make the entire trunk and window appear to be undamaged. Without anyone noticing.

Taking a deep breath, the pinch in my side from my still-healing ribs making me hiss, I closed my eyes and tried to centre myself. My eyes flew back open. Well, that was a terrible idea. Jack was weaving in and out of traffic as he increased our distance from the hospital, and I reacted poorly to the swaying of the car. Puking on the back of his seat would not help with his concentration. I gingerly shook my head to clear it before concentrating on repairing the window. Drawing in as much Universal energy as I could hold at one time, I spooled it out as tiny threads of imaginary glass, layering the illusion from the edges, working as a spider would when building her web. Gradually, the window appeared as though it was whole.

Before adjusting the damage to the trunk, I tried to ensure that our spy had not gotten closer in the past few minutes. I sent energy to the tag placed on the driver and, like sonar, I waited for the 'ping' to return. Nothing. WTF? No ping. Where did he go? Suddenly the pulse returned, not from behind us, but several lanes over to our left, flanking us. Panicking, I reached into his mind to see if he was still on target, namely us. Nothing. Feeling sorry for what was about to happen, I could sense no remaining energy I would describe as completely human. The scout had total control and had effectively wiped him back to factory default. Nothing, no memories, no independent thoughts, no identity. Mentally stepping back before my presence was noted, I released my tag and prayed the Ferin had not spotted it.

"Jack, there is about to be an accident on your left. We need to get off of this highway, now."

Trusting Jack to find the next ramp and a way to get to it without interference, I returned to my task. With the window illusion in place, I set about applying hints of colour to the rear panels, slowly building on top of one another until I cloaked the entire area in a manner I hoped had been subtle enough to not catch anyone's eye. Cloaking only really works if no one is trying to see through it. And magick only holds as long as the spell-caster stays focused. One job, Steph. You have one job right now.

Jack made his way to the right lane, threading through traffic to exit the highway just as the Ferin assassin pulled the plug on her control of the man and his vehicle. The ensuing crash added more victims to the carnage total left behind us. We had narrowly survived their manufactured suicide and the wreckage that ensued. Luck better be with us while we looked for somewhere to ditch our ride and hide out for a few hours.

Grief washed over me and out of the corner of my eye, the cloaking shimmered. Shit! Stay focused, dammit! One job, remember?

We drove through the back streets, looking for an empty warehouse. Anywhere the car could disappear, preferably in a burst of flames. For a city of its size, the area was suspiciously void of derelict buildings. Finally, he doused the headlights, and I quickly extended my cloak to cover the whole car, changing the colour at the same time. I was too tired to maintain it for long, but for the moment, we were as good as invisible.

"Are you good to move? Can you walk?" Jack asked as he stretched the kinks out of his shoulders. The fatigue of the day marked his eyes as he looked back towards the orange glow and strobing lights on the highway.

Both are excellent questions. Assessing my physical condition, I felt confident I had a good ten minutes of energy left and told Jack so.

"Drop the cloaking then. Let someone find the car. It should be a few hours before anyone notices it there."

Jack grabbed the backpacks and pulled out our clothes. Back in our leathers, we dropped the stolen scrubs into the nearest bin. A smile creased his face, and proving himself my hero once again, Jack handed me half of a mangled sandwich from the depths of his bag. It was nothing you would find in a fine restaurant but it was much needed.

Partially sated, I drew the spellwork back into my core and returned the surplus to its source. It would make things easier, quicker sometimes, to use Universal energy to give myself a boost. Apparently, the only boost I got is my ability to heal at a rapid rate. Every other personal use ends with me passed out cold. Which is not helpful when you are trying to escape from alien thugs. I can direct energy to help others, guide it to do things that are, in essence, helpful to me, but not directly affecting my health or well-being. Or my mission. Sometimes it would have been nice to just tap in and let the Universe fill in the missing pieces of knowledge needed to get this book back where it belongs. But there are no shortcuts in this game. No easy answers.

We saunter along, arms around each other, a loving couple on a quiet evening stroll. Remembering that microchips are foreign to them, I looked for anything computer-based in the shop windows; smartphones, cameras, anything tech-based. There had been computerized equipment at the hospital, though it seemed antiquated compared to what we are accustomed to. As we walked a few more blocks, it became obvious this timeline had not embraced the technologies we are so familiar with, dependent on. Yet the year is so fantastic I expected flying cars and robots everywhere.

Telephone booths stand on street corners, store signs glow with the softness only neon can provide, and the people on the sidewalks are curiously empty-handed. With something close to awe, I realize that this dimension has not become tethered to the technological advances so prevalent in the digital age, and has instead chosen to take a different path, remaining true to the analog components and simpler developments. This will make our travels both easier and harder at the same time. Locating transportation we can 'liberate' is a snap. Doing research and finding our way around will require us to back up several decades in our thinking. What we consider commonplace is not so here. We will be limited to resources that can only be found in a library or newspaper archive, and that means we will need to expose ourselves to the local population just to learn more about where we are and how to move on in our quest.

As the danger to our security weighs on me, Jack pulls me in closer and mind-speaks.

'Cop ahead. Stay cool.'

I had been so internally focused we could have walked right on by and I would have missed him. Strike two for the galactic warrior and her ability to detect threats. Sheesh.

Never one to take the easy way, Jack steers us toward the police officer and decides that striking up a conversation is an excellent way to stay under the radar. Some days I could just kill him…

Tired of Running

"Good evening, officer. How are you on this beautiful night?"

"Very fine, thank you, sir. Where are the two of you heading tonight?"

"We have just come to your fair city and are trying to get a feel for the streets."

The officer looked confused, and then suspicious. In attempting to deflect attention, Jack has forgotten to keep the slang to a minimum. Our 'English' is about to land us in trouble —again.

English is the language we think and speak in, no matter the timeline or place we end up in, but it is not always heard as we say it. Sometimes, little things become lost in the translation. Even better, it would help if one of us spoke another language. Like most tourists, we can get by in French or some smattering of Spanish, but nothing that will make us speak like a local. I always intend to learn more than the basics, but getting shot at takes priority over finding out how to sound like we belong.

So we try to speak clearly and keep profanity out of it.

My mind drifts from the conversation, my hunger and fatigue dropping me into a trance-like state and memories of past encounters swim to the surface as I lean on Jack's shoulder for support.

'Stephanie.'

"Stephanie!"

"I am so sorry, Jack. I just —" Not sure of what was going on around me, I leaned more heavily into him as if I could barely stand. Not much of an exaggeration after the day we have had.

"Officer, my wife needs to rest. Could you recommend a quiet hotel close by?"

I will ask Jack about the lost minutes when we are alone. For now, I continue to make myself as small of a threat as possible. It used to bother me that people would underestimate my strength and my abilities. Learning to mask my displeasure at being dismissed by males of all races and species has become a valuable skill. I am so often the surprise factor in a battle that Jack counts on the look of disbelief on our assailants' faces as the cue that I have joined the fight.

Tonight, my acting skills are in full swing. I pulled my energy in close and the officer soon loses interest in me, placing me firmly in the 'non-threatening' category. Addressing Jack, he gives us directions to a small, but not seedy, hotel, prone to accepting visitors in the middle of the night. I am intrigued. Just how many middle-of-the-night-visitors has this officer met up with? Trying not to be obvious, I almost let my curiosity get the better of me. Pressure on my shoulder was Jack's subtle reminder that he would take me out if I started drawing attention back to us, now that we were no longer interesting.

'I wasn't going to do anything,' I whined in Jack's head.

'Oh, no. Of course, you weren't. It never occurred to you to snoop in his head and see what he meant about "visitors."' Jack internally shook his head at me. His ability to carry on an internal and external conversation at the same time, and not cross them up, amazes me. Having run out of topics to banter about, Jack thanked the officer and we headed off, ambling down the sidewalk towards the hotel. Something twigged for me, though, a slight ripple in the night air. Jack felt it too, for I sensed his upper body tighten as he loosened his grip on me, giving me room to swing down and out of his reach should trouble start.

We had no intention of staying at the hotel, but it would be suspicious if we did not at least check in. Feeling the officer's gaze on us, Jack scouted the area as cautiously as he could. My job was to scan the side streets and small businesses as we passed. Without the technological haze that we are so used to in our own timeline, the energy readings here were crisp and sharp, almost too easy to decipher. Uncertain if the unfamiliar environment was making us paranoid or if we were actually being watched, I sent out wave after wave of sensory sonar. For the first three blocks, nothing unusual appeared. Two energies in that room, sleeping. Three small ones over there. One tired energy, deep in the alley. This was about the time when I realized I had found no animal signatures in my sweeps. No dogs, cats, or birds. No gerbils in cages. Weird… Not even rats in the alleys. My intrigue was becoming a swirling mass of questions with no ready answers.

Taking the last turn in our set of directions, Jack released my shoulder and brought his hand down to the hilt of the knife cached just inside his jacket. His level of readiness alarmed me, but there was no time to shroud our approach to the office. Someone had called ahead. Standing in the doorway, the manager waved us closer before speaking. Jack gently pushed me behind by a half step and reached out to take the man's hand. Hidden from view, I scanned the man's energy and found nothing amiss. In fact, I found nothing at all. It was like he didn't feel or think about anything, just did. Got up, ran his hotel, went to bed. Like a robot in a human skin.

'Jack. Something is not right here. I feel trapped.'

'Same here. Keep watching him. I'll sort out a room, but we need an escape plan.'

As before, Jack went through the pleasantries and greetings, claiming I was too exhausted to make small talk. After forging our names, Jack rummaged through his pockets, hoping to find some cash. Oops. This could be embarrassing, not suspicious at all. Travelling through the night, on foot, with no money. And a cop that knows where we went.

"Oh, my God! Where is your wallet, honey?!" This sounds like the normal response for a female, trying to make sense of the misfortune. "Don't tell me you dropped it? How will we ever find it? I don't know where we are?!?" Adding some hysteria tends to make people forget the situation and try to calm me down, but there was a perplexed look on the proprietor's face. I silently reviewed my words but found nothing odd in the statements, nothing that would cause this reaction.

My turn to screw up. English slang got me again. How many times have you said "Oh my God!" in everyday conversation? People understand what you mean. It doesn't imply that you are calling on God, only the level of frustration you have reached to that point. It is a very pliable phrase. If you are in a timeline where religion is a thing. If you are, however, in a timeline where God never existed, this would be a strange thing to say. How did I leap to this conclusion? All the little pieces had finally fallen into place.

Take the year. We are used to saying '2019' when we all know it means '2019 A.D.'. The Year of our Lord. After his death. What if none of that ever happened? What if someone just started recording the history of the human race as it unfolded, began at the beginning and we are now in the year 4781? No Christmas or Easter. No Heaven. Certainly no Hell. Just existence. You live. You die. And your spirit, with no previously arranged destination, wanders around being lost and confused until it just 'winks out' when the energy is gone. With no unifying place to go and no belief system in place, souls just dissipate and vanish from this world. How do humans live a life without a gathering place, without the hope of something beyond this meagre existence? After more than a century of seeking answers, there is a fundamental need for the belief in a power greater than ourselves, in an expectation of an afterlife.

Words kept falling from my mouth, hoping to deflect the manager. I continued babbling nonsense while Jack kept looking for cash (that he didn't have) and his wallet (that he wasn't carrying). For my grand finale, I resorted to the feminine 'ace-in-the-hole'—I started the waterworks. Heaving sobs mixed with disjointed statements about wanting to experience the big city, how we had travelled so far, and that we just needed to sleep for a little while, but our car was stolen, and now our money was gone. At least compassion was still alive and well. Or he was just so embarrassed by my display that he couldn't take the influx of emotion I was pushing at him as the tears streamed down my face. Checking his records, the manager grabbed a key from behind the counter and led us to a small room in the back.

"Just be gone by sunrise so my boss doesn't find out," he said, as he turned to go back to his office.

No worries there. We'd be gone as soon as his lights went out.

Jack did his usual reconnaissance. Not much to see in a twelve-by-twelve room with a bath, but it makes him feel prepared. When he gave me the all-clear, I went into the bathroom to dry my face and use the facilities. It always amazes me how long you can hold it when there are no other options. Once the option is there though, man, did I need to go. Jack too. He started banging on the door almost immediately, accusing me of hogging the room. I briefly considered being childish, but wrapped up my business and gave him some privacy while I checked the window for surveillance. Nothing. My sensory scan picked up four other guests, all sleeping. The hotel manager was still awake, though. Leaving may not be so simple.

Thinking we should take advantage of our precious sanctuary, I turn back towards the room to see Jack, passed out on the bed. He is always so strong; it hits me in the heart when he shows his vulnerable side. I am tempted to watch over him, to be the protector, but logic pulls me to lie down beside him and I curled up in his arms, safe for this moment in time. Fatigue washed over me and my eyelids, heavier than I remembered, fluttered closed.

A Masterful Strike

Some natural force let Jack know it was the final hour before dawn, the time of stealthy getaways. Hitting snooze on an internal alarm clock only works if it's your internal clock. Hitting Jack to keep him in bed was not an option. He likes it rough. And we didn't have time for fun and games. As he slipped out from beneath the covers, I took a moment to gaze at his well-formed body, noting the scars he carries, the slight stiffness in his left hip. He would never blame me for that, even though he should. Jack was in perfect condition before he met me on that riverbank. If he hadn't chosen to protect me that night, he would have been more alert when the attack came at him. And it wasn't even the vampire that did the damage. That would be the rock he fell onto while trying to pull me along beside him on the narrow brush path.

After his subtle warning, and after I failed at decapitating him, Jack decided to run rather than fight. When I stumbled onto the vampire, Jack had been following this demon for more than a year, always a step behind the carnage. He worked in solitude, hiding the carnage under the guise of animal attacks or accidents. People will always believe the simplest explanation, leading to the slaughter of many a bear or wolf who had done nothing but be in the wrong place.

Running from an elemental being like a vampire is tricky at best, impossible for an amateur like me. Jack quickly realized I was strong enough to fight, possessed some skills (not perfect, for which he was grateful), and had the desire to live. Being semi-immortal, I often take risks that are on the edge of suicidal. As we rushed along, the branches grabbed at our clothes and made more noise than we needed. I disentangled myself and got my head in the game. I may not have fought such a creature before, but I am a quick study. Getting a firmer grip on my sword, I pulled my hand free just as we rounded a tight corner, a much better position to provide a defence. The unforeseen circumstance was Jack overcompensating and landing awkwardly, colliding with the aforementioned rock, and losing the feeling in his leg.

I have to admit that I panicked when I saw him fall. I was planning to help him in battle, not protect him against an enemy I knew nothing about. Mist and shadow were all I had seen to this point, filled with foreboding, like death approaching on his dark horse. Jack yelled at me to turn, and I spun on my heel, sword swinging through in a powerful arc, connecting with nothing. From the darkness came a deep, guttural chuckle, mirthless and chilling. Backing away, I stumbled and stepped off of the bank, tumbling into the bone-chilling water of the river.

"Stay where you are. Stay in the water!" Jack hollered from his position on the riverbank.

"What!" Fearing I would lose my footing on the slick rocks or freeze to death, I was madly scrabbling for the edge.

"Stay in the running water. Don't get drawn to him."

Confused, I continued to reach for Jack, but the fog swept across the ground between us. My mouth dried up, my lungs constricted. I had never felt fear so pervasive, so consuming. I just wanted it to stop.

"Come to me, child."

The words slid through the air as though they could slip between the molecules, bending everything in their path to his will. I felt myself responding to the power he exuded. Still hidden within the shadows, with no solidity of form, I found no target to fix on. And that voice oozed into my brain like a hit of heroin, begging for more of it, no matter the risk.

Jack, sensing I was in deep trouble, and not just from the water, struggled to get to his feet, forcing his damaged leg to respond. Gritting his teeth through the pain, he called out a challenge, man-to-whatever a vampire is considered to be.

"Are you actually going to stoop to attacking a weak little thing like that? After all these years, after all your training, that's all you've got?" A little thick on the bravado, if you ask me, but men are men, and not programmed to let such talk go on by. The vampire turned towards Jack, and while I could not see his grin, I could feel it. I focused on that image, wrapped it up in my mind and pictured where the rest of him would (or should) be if he were solid. My feet, ice-cold in the river, would not hold me much longer and Jack was injured. I straightened up, rolled my shoulders, and prepared to engage in a battle I had no business being in. Though I had never fought a vampire before, I was fairly certain he had never matched swords with a witch, either.

Drawing up as much energy as I could hold, I pushed his influence from my thoughts, centring only on his grin. I had never resisted so much power before, and the strain was intense. The vampire felt it, too. His grin began to slowly melt into a sneer as he turned to face me.

"So, little witch. You think you can best me. You have not got the skills, my dear."

"Maybe not," I replied with a sneer of my own. "But he does."

As the vampire realized he had placed himself between the two of us, he briefly took his eyes off of me to seek out Jack. That was all we needed. The sound of two swords cutting through the air sent shivers through my body as the rush of energy followed my sword along its arc. Severing the space where his neck should have been, his essence cascaded out to fill the void in the in-between spaces, making him solid enough for the blade Jack raised to pierce his heart. With a cry of mortal agony, the life the vampire had once lived returned to him, along with all the sins of his immortal, and immoral, life. Jack held his sword in place until the body of the once-man crumbled to dust and drifted down onto the moving water to float away like the fallen leaves of the trees.

I fell to my knees in the mud of the riverbank, my chest heaving, reaching for Jack to make sure he was alive. With a surge of inhuman strength, Jack stretched his hands to the sky as he made his way to his feet. He let loose a battle cry that crawled across my skin and buried in my ears, ringing and echoing his victory for the valley to hear. Collapsing beside me, he gasped for air, laughing and sounding manic. Unsure of what Jack was experiencing, I withdrew my hand and backed away slowly.

"'Little witch.' Well, he didn't know you very well, did he?" Jack chuckled as he sat up and met my wary gaze.

"What are you?" I demanded. "You are no more human than he was, are you?"

Jack's face went stony. "I am well trained, with a little magick thrown in for good measure. You are not what you seem either. There is much mystery about you, much more I would like to learn about."

After my evening of adventure, I was not in the mood for banter. Standing tall, I lost my temper on this stranger who had both saved and endangered my life all in the last hour. When I ran out of insults and before I resorted to cursing the man, Jack stood toe to toe with me and had the audacity to kiss me on the tip of my nose.

Sweeping his arm as if he were proffering a plumed hat, he backed away gingerly, favouring his left leg, and parted with no more than a glimmer of moonlight to mark his passing.

Suddenly bereft, and utterly exhausted, not to mention cold from the waist down, I stumbled up the path, seeking shelter for the remaining hours before dawn. Shivering in the dampening air, I rubbed my bare skin to regain some warmth.

"You are welcome to join me, bruja." His voice, smooth as silk, whispered out on the wind as though carried like the down of a thistle.

Startled, I lurched back, my arms flailing, colliding with the hardness of his chest. Finding him within my reach, I spun and struck out at him, still angry over the way he had caused so much chaos. At least that was the way I was seeing it.

My fist was met with chuckling and the slightest wisp of air as he anticipated my reaction.

"That was solid. Or, it would have been."

My temper peaked. Cold, wet, hungry, tired, not a pleasant combination on my best day. Pulling back to try again, I found myself staring at the stars, taken out at the ankles with a sweep that I should have been able to prevent, had I been cool and collected.

"I like the temper. Now use it wisely."

His voice floating through the dimly lit branches angered me further. Gathering energy into a tight ball, I took a deep breath and put all other thoughts aside. The set of my shoulders announced an attack using my physical form. Time for a surprise or two of my own.

Drifting on the wind came the one thing I was waiting for —
his aura. As he became more confident, it surged out ahead of
him, glowing in a hue of yellow so delicate it could have been
dust freshly fallen from fairy wings. I inhaled and oriented
on the colour, rather than the body it encompassed. When
I felt its edge brush against mine, I exhaled, surrounding his
energy with my own before compacting his aura in tightly
and driving the very air from his body.

As he fell to the ground, gasping, he reached up with a smile.
Not wanting to harm him, I released my grip and let the energy
melt back into the Earth just as Jack passed out from the
pressure. A 'little' witch indeed. Like I often say, what's the
point of having skills if you can't use them to help people?
Here, it helped me feel a whole lot better.

It was no small task to drag Jack back into the brush where
he had started a small fire. He is built for adventure, power
and brute strength. None of that makes him manoeuvrable
when unconscious. Depleted and overwhelmed with fatigue,
I banked the fire and collapsed beside him, each keeping the
other warm through the break of dawn.

A Darkening Wood

Another dawn, another day.

"Oh, Stephanie…"

"Hmmmmm?"

"Wake up, dammit."

"When are we?" You know our travels are wearing thin when I wake up asking 'when' and not 'where'. The where doesn't seem as impactful anymore. You figure out the where, then you work with what is at hand. The when is often more important, and in this intergalactic scavenger hunt we have fallen into, solving the 'when' gets us moving onto the next phase of the chase.

"Still in 4781, as near as I can tell." Jack's voice came to me from behind the door of the hotel refrigerator, where he was scrounging for anything small enough to take with us. Tossing a package of crackers in my direction, he proceeded to the bathroom for his morning ablutions.

Getting out of bed, I moved to the window to see if we had brought any more attention to ourselves. The flickering neon of the hotel signs glowed faintly in the early morning light. Weird. I couldn't hear any birdsong in the trees. Being in the city doesn't stop birds from singing, at least not on the Earth I know. Yet another reminder that we are not in Kansas anymore, Toto. Jack came to stand behind me. I leaned into his strength, drawing on it to bolster my own, and sent him the healing he needed. Jack nuzzled my neck in thanks for the gift before turning me in his arms. His kiss warmed me to my toes. I curled them in the carpet and reached up to pull him to me. As the world dropped away, we pretended we were the only two people on the planet, with no agenda, no schedule, no bounty on our heads.

Bang. Bang. Bang. The sudden pounding on the door broke our embrace and the mood. Sigh...

"Who is it?" Jack asked as we hurriedly flanked the door.

"You need to get moving," the hotel manager replied. "You can't be here when my boss arrives."

"How long do we have?" Stuffing some stale crackers in my mouth, I began gathering what little we had strewn about the room, making sure the Book was secured, along with the scraps grabbed during our escape from the hospital.

"Ten minutes at most. Hurry. I don't want to lose my job for you two." The manager scurried back to his office, Jack watching him through the slit in the curtains.

Curious, I peeked out too, but nothing seemed to be amiss. Maybe, just maybe, we had found a good guy who wanted to do a good thing for a pair of strangers in need.

Jack closed the door behind us and scanned the area as we moved off, away from the main road, melting into the brush behind the hotel. Setting off at a pace reserved for marathon trainers, we jogged along the edge of the trail, having no idea where it led. Our footsteps pounded softly in the morning dampness, disturbing leaves as we passed. Stride for stride, we fell into a mated rhythm as the miles disappeared behind us. Still within the wilds of this planet, we looked for signs of habitation. The small shards of debris humans inevitably leave in their wake. Surely, the city we left behind was not all that existed. But I saw nothing. Not one cigarette butt, not one soda can, not one piece of paper or plastic bag. More weirdness.

Even stranger, the woods we travelled through seemed to open before us as we ran. If we slowed up, the opening did the same. Jack and I changed our run to a walk and then stopped. I looked behind us to see how far we had come. At least I would have if the trail had still been there. I watched as the trees closed in and the very path our feet had touched vanished as though it had never been. Quickly, I turned to see the trees before us doing the same thing. In a panic, we raced ahead, forcing the opening to stay that way. Looking up to orient to the sun, Jack gradually turned us through the bush, angling away from the centre it had led us into.

We pounded through the forest, keeping our shift as subtle as possible, our energy depleting as we ran. My limited intake was showing. I fell behind. Jack cut the pace to keep in step with me, all the time watching the sky for signs to indicate the edge of the forest. In time, a thinning of the trees appeared, and we hurried to reach it before the trap was sprung.

Magick in its most natural form. The planet protecting itself from intruders. The trees, its guardians. Raw magick. The sheer power of it was intimidating, making us feel small, reminding me we do not control our environment.

Gasping for breath, we collapsed on the edge of the forest, monitoring the underbrush, watching for signs that the trees were still trying to prevent our departure. The grass whispered, though no wind blew, and I strained to hear the message. It was the only sound not our own. I heard not one bird. Not even the hum of an insect. How did this planet exist without animal life, beyond humans? How did humans exist without other wildlife? There had to be more we just weren't seeing, that the planet would not allow us to witness. Perhaps the area surrounding the city had been expunged, removing all insects, which would affect the bird and reptile population and then the predators. But it was so strange. I didn't miss mosquitoes as we huddled in the meadow, but the near-total silence was making me edgy.

It must have been affecting Jack too, as I could sense him reaching out to find something, anything, any information about the planet and its inhabitants. He sat quietly, taking stock of where we were and what we had to work with. From prior experience, we would not get out of this timeline until we figured out the mystery and found the next piece of the riddle. The Book doesn't give free advice on the mysteries, or what the goal is in each time jump. In fact, the Book never gives up anything it doesn't have to. It has been a fight the whole time.

A multitude of questions cross my mind almost daily. Why not give it up, let someone else solve the mystery, translate the text? Why keep fighting at all? When is enough, enough? I probably would have walked away years ago, but Jack keeps me in the game. That and the ever-present awareness about the Council's plans to use the Book and its power to rule every galaxy they set foot in. They are not the good guys.

So, here we sit, contemplating the might of the Universe, the strangeness of the worlds we find ourselves in, and how we are supposed to get out of this mess.

"We're going to have to return to the city." Jack finally stated, having weighed every conceivable option.

"Now? Or at dusk?"

"Better start now. We need daylight to make progress, and I can't tell how far we have come, having to take that path through the woods."

It sounds like a plan, or at least the beginnings of one, with one minor problem. Which way is back to town? Jack arrived at the same realization, for he got to his feet and turned in a tight circle, looking for signs of industry, of people and habitation. Our peaceful meadow suddenly seemed like a trap, after all. In every direction beyond the grass's edge, the forest stood silently, brooding over our movements. I could sense the collective thoughts of the woods. There was a definite strategy in place, and we would not escape so easily this time.

Scanning the trees for signs of weakness, I noticed the tiniest of glimmers within the branches. Each time I set eyes on them fully, they blinked out, only to appear a few feet away, never collected together, always in motion. Using my peripheral vision instead, I tried to focus on one area of the forest without drawing attention to what I was doing.

'Jack,' I mind-messaged him. *'There's something at the edge of the woods behind you. I think we might have a guide or two in there.'*

Jack swung his head around, always in protection mode. His motion startled the lighted beings, and they winked out.

'Slowly. Look without staring. They're skittish.'

'You think,' Jack can use sarcasm as fluidly as I can. *'You could've added that.'*

True enough. I was not used to our telepathic link and its speed. I had barely thought the words when he reacted. Note to self: Lead with the vital stuff next time.

We settled back down into the grass and pretended not to be looking. Jack fidgeted as time passed, his anxiety reaching new levels. Truthfully, I was thinking we had scared them off for good when one, then another light flashed. Trying to focus with the edges of your eyes makes the rest of your vision soften. It's the best way to see energy and auras, so we have had lots of practice, but it took these beings to show us the way to get through the woods.

With our peripheral gaze locked on the lights, the trees in front of us shifted out of focus. You know the saying, can't see the forest, blah, blah, blah. Here it was in full colour, or should I say, in shades of colour. The aura of the trees morphed into a blur of greens through which a clearly defined path appeared, a ley line the trees did not cross or grow within. The route was thin. Only one person could pass at a time, but there was a delicately lit starting point.

Taking a moment to rest, Jack and I began to 'talk' through the logistics of this journey. Jack always likes to have a battle plan. I think better under stress, even duress. Our differences make our team work. After gathering our things and our thoughts, we stood at the edge of the glade, and Jack softened his gaze. Eye strain could become a serious problem, so we would take turns scanning for the path, while the other stayed tight on their shoulder. Switching roles would be a challenge, but for the start, Jack would take the lead while I guarded the rear.

Before we step into the shadows, I gave a nod and a silent thank you to the beings who had helped us, whether or not it was their intention. I still don't know what they were. Maybe fairies, maybe angels, maybe they were nothing more than fireflies, that insects did exist here. I wasn't about to grab one to satisfy my curiosity. Taking Jack's elbow, we moved off into the gloom, following the faintest of energy trails, hoping it was not another clever trap.

Darkness enveloped us. The branches touched overhead, obscuring our view of the sky and any indication of the passage of time. It became oppressive within the towering trees, our steps taken with great care so as to keep to the ley line, switching places whenever the path widened slightly. We relied on each other for guidance, and finding no challenge in the rear, closed our eyes when in the following position, night vision a precious necessity when in the lead. The strain of the journey became evident as we pushed on, not knowing if there was an end to reach or if this would be the end of the chase.

My mind wandered as we walked, dredging up thoughts and memories in a jumbled mess. Occasionally, I took time to curse the blasted Book I had so gallantly agreed to protect. And for what? So we could be consumed by man-suffocating trees? Thirst, hunger, and exhaustion do strange things to your brain. Sensing a sanity slip approaching, I latched onto the puzzle we had been working on prior to landing on this planet. It's funny how you can continue with the task at hand while simultaneously thinking about something completely unrelated. Or something reminiscent. Like the time we were fleeing from the French police. Not the Legionnaires this time, the actual police in Paris. Guess they didn't like us breaking into the Louvre.

Our French Connection

The updated security protocols might have something to do with our visit. And it's not like we didn't give the painting back. We just couldn't read the clue on the back while it was hanging on the wall. Jack had our escapade planned down to the nanosecond, each guard's position, how fast we could run, when the elevators were shut off, the rotation of the artwork. We spent weeks looking at every aspect of the museum, trying to prepare for any hiccup. In the end, the job was riskier than it should have been, with a guard stopping to admire a piece in the gallery backing onto the one our painting hung in.

Jack positioned himself behind a statue, hiding within the shadows while he waited for the guard to make his rounds. For three weeks, the guard had faithfully made the circuit in fourteen minutes, giving Jack time to get in, remove the art piece from the frame, and get out of the museum. (I am not telling how we got in. Trade secrets and all that. Plus, we may need to break in again someday. The Book doesn't care about synchronicity.) On that day, the guard opted to extend his study of a sculpture, messing up Jack's meticulous plan, throwing the timing right out the window. In fact, out the window was where I stood waiting for Jack to lower the painting to me, and my presence would soon gather attention of its own. One simply does not linger outside of the Louvre in the dead of the night with good intentions. My 'costume' deterred a few locals out for a lovers' stroll, but the local constabulary would not appreciate me holding down the street corner for much longer.

Not knowing what caused the delay, and having no way to find out, I slowly sauntered from my position and pretended to adjust my garments. Loosening my corset, I slipped my knife into my palm, then walked along the sidewalk, keeping an eye out for drunks, braggarts, and cops. Forgetting my garb was eye-catching to the right 'clientele', I stepped out of my role as I ran scenarios, trying to figure out what I could do to help. Since I didn't know the situation inside, this was truly an exercise in futility, but I couldn't stop myself. Standing in the shadows, I tried to appear small and indistinct. Right then, three things happened. One: a man approached me, hoping to 'buy some time'. Two: one of Paris's finest spotted the two of us and began shouting for us to move off. And three: Jack came racing around the corner with the painting rolled up under his arm.

The ensuing chaos is hard to describe. My unwanted attention seeker vanished when the commotion started, not wanting to get arrested for his interest. The officer, not immediately certain what was going on, couldn't decide if he should chase the john, question me about my activities, or figure out why Jack was running through the streets. I don't think he had even seen the painting at this point. That was about to change.

Added to the mix was the security guard from the Louvre. As Jack explained later, the delay in the guard's routine meant that Jack could not sneak onto the top of the elevator in time to ride back up to the roof deck when the guards switched floors. Forced to decide, and with the painting already cut from its frame, Jack escaped through the museum and walked out the back door. Sometimes looking like you belong can work in your favour. This time, the deception bought him a few seconds as the guards were unaware of his presence until the door closed behind him and the click of the lock alerted them to his departure.

As Jack rounded the corner and came face to face with the cop who was thinking he should question me, I turned towards the officer, knife in hand, waving it wildly to get his attention. Jack, realizing he needed to find another route, ducked behind my slashing hand and sped off into the shadows of the alley. Next to join the party is the museum guard, who slammed into the constable, both being caught off balance and hitting the sidewalk. This was my cue to scramble off as well, heading in the opposite direction, hoping to draw one of them away from Jack. In the end, the two lawmen, entangled as they were, lost track of us both. We took a very circuitous means to return to our refuge, winded and unscathed. For the record, it is not easy to flee in high heels and full skirts.

We spent the next two days in hiding, certain of our arrest were we to appear during daylight hours. The night was our friend, giving us shadows to slink in. Jack stole a newspaper from a neighbouring apartment and scanned the articles for any report of the theft. Nothing. But the increased presence of officers on the street below meant they were still looking for somebody, probably us. We spent our time reading and re-reading the page in The Book that was revealed when the artwork was near. Hours slipped away while we deciphered the clues it gave us, matching every tiny piece to an answer found in or on the painting. The work was time-consuming, mentally draining, and frustrating. What little we have learned so far seems to be a mix of thoughts and concerns about the changes in the author's society and ideas about where the Universe is heading. There are glimpses of more detailed magickal writings, but The Book is never openly obvious about what it wants us to know. And there is no skipping ahead either. The pages were blank until it made the clue known. Each piece opens up a new section of the puzzle. And I still don't know what picture is on the box.

These safety checks ensure the magick in this missive will not be used by any ordinary human. While we have yet to decipher more than a few chapters, the power behind the spells it contains is at a Universal level, and probably should not have been recorded, to begin with. But some over-achieving angel thought it would be safe enough, and besides, people can't read Enochian or Atlantean, so what's the harm? Angels can be a tad narrow-minded. Humans might not understand their language, but modern computers are whizzes at analyzing codes, and languages are just that. Our new age of technology threatens the secrecy of The Book, the Angelic realm, maybe even the Universe, if they hid the secrets of creation within these pages. This is what the Council so desperately wants. The ability to create life itself. The power to populate worlds, galaxies, universes. All enthralled to their leadership, their way of life. All created without the desire for free will, choice, or rebellion. In opposition to their tyranny, stands the Assembly and its Ambassadors. Our goal is to find these relics first and protect them, and with them, humanity.

Simulation

While my brain travelled its own path, around us the gloom has lightened. The outer edge of the forest is within reach. What lies beyond, we cannot yet see, but hope is a tenuous emotion. The spots of light faded from our vision as the ley line dissipated back to the ground. We cautiously stepped into the city outskirts within sight of the hotel we fled from earlier. Back in civilization, loosely termed of course, for not all about this place is civilized.

Ours needs are simple: water, food, rest. In that order. We have been running on empty for far too long and the battle is still ahead of us. Getting a better sense of what we are dealing with, we calmly begin walking towards the city lights. Jack takes up the rear as I search for the lines hidden beneath the concrete and asphalt of the streets and sidewalks. Not seeing them does not mean they are not there. Closing my eyes, I reach for the pulse of the planet. Humming under our feet, unknown by most, the ley lines are the planetary communication system, sending and receiving information about its health, its resources, and its capacity. It would be foolish for both of us to wander about blind to the everyday things in our path. Jack stepped in front, taking my hand in his, trusting my guidance to set us on the right road.

I gently swung my head back and forth, searching for the energy flow. Finally.

"To our left, Jack. About twelve feet."

Jack turned us in the desired direction and moved forward carefully, awaiting my next instruction. His senses were on the world around us while I concentrated on the one below our feet. Staying loose and calm, on the outside, Jack looked like an average tourist wandering the city. Inside, he was processing every fragment of movement that caught his eye, every sound, every idea that came to him. Intuition is a fluid science. The mystery is which piece of data will be the one that saves your life.

"Okay. Turn to 3:00. It looks like this line goes straight for a while. Can we go that way?"

"We're good for a few blocks. Come. Walk beside me."

Understanding that we would appear more normal walking abreast rather than in single file, I open my eyes, leaving my internal radar locked on the energetic river streaming faintly below us. Jack took my arm in his, keeping me close as lovers do. We talked, looked in windows, stopped for traffic. Basically, we did everyday things, all the while scanning and searching, seeking and monitoring. As we moved along the street, we noticed a subtle shift in the people who were visible. Checking the cars, the people in the stores, the people on the sidewalks, all middle-aged. The men were clean-shaven, all with blue eyes and blond hair. It would not take long for them to find us. Thinking back, I could not recall seeing any brunettes since we arrived in this neighbourhood. And no people with a non-white skin tone. And no children. Before I wigged out, Jack pulled me in tight and drained the anxiety off.

'Just a little farther, and we should be clear. Stay with it, lover,' Jack sent in a mind-speak.

'What the fuck is going on here? They look like clones, not individuals!'

'They do look like replications, but there are slight differences.'

'But there are no children. Where are the crying babies? Why aren't there teenagers smoking on the corner? There's nothing!'

'We don't know enough about this society to know how they handle child-rearing. There's a lot that is confusing right now. Let it go, Steph. We need to find the next ley line.'

Mentally shaking my head, I dropped back into scanning mode. But I couldn't let it go. The lack of other life forms bothered me. We're in a big city. There's no refuse — no garbage, rats, or sewer grates. The more I looked, the less I saw. The buildings were all the same style, same height, with different colours on the doors. At least they were numbered or I wouldn't be able to tell we had moved. The storefronts were all designed in the same manner, the displays all similar. I was seriously freaking out. Jack's mind appeared to be focused on our security.

As I processed all these things, Jack tensed. Responding to his cue, I snapped out of my reverie and subtly looked around.

'Ten o'clock high. Watcher in the window.'

I continued to observe the scenery as though enjoying the view. With no reason to look up, I accepted Jack's assessment and walked with him, chatting nonsense to keep up appearances. As I became more animated in my 'chatter', the sensation of eyes on us prickled my neck. The spark of tiny red lights ahead of us grabbed my attention.

'There are cameras on the corners. They just activated.'

'Copy that. Scanning for more.'

Jack dropped into his military mindset and I felt his body change to prepare for the potential battle. I can't maintain that level of readiness, so I rolled my shoulders, took a few deeper breaths and cleared my mind.

'Cameras above each door frame. Discreet. Look like light fixtures.'

'So, they watch everyone coming and going from their homes? Everything is being monitored?' Good thing we didn't have to speak to communicate. I was certain they were capturing every word we spoke, too. Hopefully, my gibberish was confusing them.

'I don't remember seeing cameras in the other part of town. Is this area different somehow? It seems like a higher security section. Everything is limited. What things look like. How many people. What can be here. And we definitely do not belong.'

I was getting a grim feeling about the monitoring and what it meant. You would think I had learned not to think negatively. How many decades now? Seriously. No sooner had I gone to that darker place when a phalanx of officers appeared on the street. Jack also spotted them and his arm dropped until we were simply holding hands. He squeezed it to make sure I was aware of his intentions. My return squeeze let him know I would follow his lead.

"Honey, I think we should check out that bridal shop we saw a few blocks back. Do you mind going back for a minute?" I even added the bride-to-be syrup to my voice, hoping to be more convincing.

Jack blinked before replying. "But that's the third one today. Haven't you seen every dress already?" Typical boyfriend whine before capitulation.

"They might have something different. Please. It will only take a few minutes." A little lean and a pleading look as Jack turned his face to mine.

'Ready?'

'Yup, which direction?'

'Turn back when I agree to go with you. Take the first right, go down two blocks, then hang another right. I want to draw them out and come around behind them.'

'Copy that.'

"We'll be late for our lunch meeting if we take too long. Can you make it quick?" spoken with the tone of an indulgent but frustrated male, appealing to his partner's wishes.

"Oh, thank you, honey!" I gave him a big hug as we turned back to 'go check the shop'. Picking up the pace to match the hurry Jack had included in his statement, we arrived at the corner and ducked down to the right. As we cleared the front of the building, Jack took off at a run, with me pounding the pavement behind him. If we weren't getting their attention before, this would certainly do it.

As we neared the last corner, a tiny glimmer on our left caught my eye. Recognizing it as kinfolk to our helpers in the forest, I grabbed Jack's arm and pulled him with me as I called *'Left!'* in his head. I have to give him credit—he never broke stride or asked a question. Trust is such a valuable thing in any relationship, but when the chips are down, the bond is vital. Before us, a small slit between buildings opened up, barely wide enough for us to squeeze through. Placing our lives in the hands of the little folk, we scurried into the gap, and I prayed we had made the right choice, for there was no going back now. Literally. As we moved away from the sidewalk, the bricks closed in behind us as the pathway opened in front. Forced to move in the only direction left to us, I stepped toward the strangely fluid wall that we faced. Feeling trapped in much the same way as we had in the forest, Jack and I kept in tight formation as we walked. With only the glow from the beacon which led us in here, we felt our way through the darkness, pushing against the 'building', watching the molecules flow out of our way only to regroup behind us. Being this close to the light source, I saw they were indeed small entities, slightly larger than fireflies, and more sentient if their help to us was any indication.

Feeling claustrophobic, Jack and I spread apart, pushing against the walls to test their solidity. Everything we reached for moved out of our grasp, giving us no more information about its construction, keeping its secrets. Each answer gave us more questions, and my mind buzzed with the possibilities. Feeling a little on the crazy side, I was about to ask the 'fireflies' what they were and where they were leading us. Weird shit happens when you are exhausted. Perhaps this entire episode is a dream. Maybe I'll wake up and be in my own bed, curled up with Jack and a glorious day ahead of us to do absolutely nothing. I can't even recall the last time I had a day like that. I'm not sure Jack knows how to 'do nothing.'

More lights collected before us, brightening the path and pushing back the walls. A wavering of the structures became apparent, the edges shimmering as we passed by. The glow intensified as the ley line we were approaching lit up like a runway, and the buildings vanished into the dark behind us. Blinded by the sudden influx of light, we covered our eyes until they adjusted. Turning around slowly, we marvelled at the internal edifice we had entered. We had our answers. But it didn't look like I would be getting food any time soon. This was going to be a long day.

Finding Freedom

"How in God's name are we supposed to survive this? Does God even exist here? Lord knows we're not going to exist for long. Even if we were to find food, it won't do us any good! Humans aren't designed to live on bits and bytes. No wonder there were no animals or trash. How in the fuck did we end up in a simulation!! This is Universally uncool!" I continued to rant on this topic for quite some time while Jack turned his impressive skills to better use. I'm pretty sure I made up new swear words before my tirade ran its course.

Trying not to cry, I slumped to the floor and held my head in my hands. I have been hungry before. I have been thirsty before. And I have gone for days without sleep. But I have always known that each of those things was available, I just had to find it. Now, I have been thrown into a place where two of those things are not likely to show up. Realizing I was close to losing it, I melted myself the rest of the way down to the floor and lay there, not moving, not thinking. Jack, sensing this was a breaking point for me, pulled me into a tight embrace, all the while sending out soothing thoughts. My despair engulfed us both as he drew it into himself to lessen the wave of emotions I was drowning in.

Stroking my hair, his finger bumping over the tangles, Jack thought through our current dilemma before offering his opinion.

"The primary question is this: Is the whole thing a simulation? Or only this section of the city? The hospital and that entire event were too real to be 'fake', you know what I mean? And the cars, the shootout, the Ferin. I think we are working with two realities here, laid parallel to each other, and we keep crossing the line between 'real' and 'not-so-much'".

"So, there could be actual food out there?" My stomach cried 'Mutiny!' and I scrambled to my feet, hope bringing stamina into my overworked body.

"Slow down, Steph," Jack said, placing his palms to my chest. "It's just a theory. I need to talk it out some more."

"Can we walk and talk?" I would not sit here when a cheeseburger was within reach. I wanted one so badly I could smell it, almost taste it. Triggering those senses brought me back to myself. You can be such a lousy witch, Stephanie DuMonde. In the flight from the city police, I had reverted to fugitive mode and forgotten all the magick at my disposal. This adventure was knocking me off my game.

Game.

This is a game.

We are in a game!

"Jack! Are we in a sim? Is it possible to be inside the programming of a computer?"

"You're asking me if it's possible? We have been to places and times that didn't exist until we got there. I would have to say 'yes', it is possible. But I think it is more than that. There's an experiment I want to try. Can you hang on while I work it out?"

Sigh. He is so polite. Internally, I am screaming "No, I'm fucking starving and I want out of this nightmare" and every other thought I have about breaking this world apart. Externally, I shrug and begin walking around our perimeter.

Leaving him to puzzle things out, I stretched my aura outwards, testing the walls that confined us, trying to find a weakness, a symbol, a stray bit of something. As I approached each segment, it moved away, flowing and rippling like a waterfall of pixels. I tried to peer closer at the bits, but they would blur and shift as if the program knew what I was trying to do. It was analyzing quicker than I could.

"Jack!" I shouted as I spun in a circle in the middle of our cavern. "Think faster. This machine is catching up to you!"

His eyes widened as he reached the same realization. We were indeed in a simulation — controlled by an artificially intelligent, soon-to-be-sentient being. The longer we stayed, the more it learned about us, and therefore how to combat our moves. Time to shake things up. Even mind-speak would be tricky. All it needed was energy, like our thoughts. How in all that is real are we supposed to create and execute an escape when thinking about it could give our plans away?

Taking a chance, Jack sent me one word—*'Chatter.'*

Chatter. Confusion. Overload. Talk as much as I could, about anything and everything not related to our journey or our mission. Simultaneously, I needed to think about totally different things to add a layer of data for the entity to sort through. Jack did the same thing. Our previously quiet space became a cacophony of noise and gibberish, none of it making sense to either of us. Underneath the misdirection, Jack gestured using military hand signals blended with sign language and some general motions that meant nothing. The combination gave me a headache.

Out of the corner of my eye, I could see a disruption in the flow of the images the AI created. As it struggled to sort out valuable data from fluff, we moved, separating ourselves just enough to force the computer to stretch out the vision, adding more details for it to manage. The more we did, the more the simulation flickered, with individual pixels flashing and disappearing, showing the world behind the curtain.

Deciding the time was as good as it was going to get, Jack and I ran at the wall in front of us, coming together to condense our final push. Grabbing my hand, Jack pulled me in tight to create a denser mass, and we catapulted ourselves at the wavering image before us.

Fireflies & Fairies

There is no pleasant way to stop when you are fleeing headlong at something that turns out to not be there when you hit it. Arms and legs tangled in a jumbled mess, we appeared to be back in the land of the living. This was not without inherent danger, but these were dangers I prepared for. In our favour, the day was nearing dusk. Sorting out our parts and pieces, we stood and dusted ourselves off, trying to be stealthy as we assessed where we were and who had seen us fall out of the wall. We might as well have been in New York City. Nobody cared. No one even commented except for the guy whose car we slammed into. And he didn't stick around. Traffic is the same everywhere. When your light is green, get going. It worked for me.

Lifting my nose skyward, I took in a deep breath and just held it for a few seconds. It's funny how you don't know what's missing until it comes back to you. The last few hours have been sterile. Not a scent or noise to be sensed. No wonder I had forgotten to use them. Inactivity had dulled them. Now, there was so much to bring in. I preferred to start with the pizza place on the next block.

"Can we have pizza, PLEASE, Jack? PLEASE?" I begged, pleading my heart out, knowing we still had one more thing to find—money. As much as I hate to stoop to criminal activity, our options were limited. Actually, options were down to one. Thinking alike, Jack subtly scanned the crowd and spotted the one person least likely to miss the money we planned to steal. He was also the least likely to be carrying cash, but cards can work too. I hope.

A little misdirect, a bump and nudge, an apology and the obligatory swipe of the jacket, and we were off. Picking a pocket is an art, perfected over the decades, though I would rather earn my money the old-fashioned way. Unfortunately, I have outlived any friends or distant relations, so I won't be inheriting anyone's fortune.

Walking to the next block with the wallet in Jack's possession, we turned the corner and continued past the pizza parlour I had smelled after we crashed this party. Not wanting to make a bee-line for it, Jack led me down the street to a small park where we could sit and admire the view. My stomach had other ideas. That mix of scents, the heady aroma of tomato sauce and pepperoni, all baked to perfection… I have to confess I was drooling a bit by this point.

Taking pity on me, we walked back up the sidewalk, looking in all the windows along the way, Jack doing surveillance, me doing my best not to clobber him, grab the money and run. Sensing my mood, he turned to me with a grin.

"Patience, grasshopper," he said with an evil grin. I slugged him.

My stomach came back to life with a roar. I was a little embarrassed standing in line. The entire restaurant tried not to look at us. Our appearance might have had a little to do with it. We weren't exactly fashion models after the last few days. Those dulled senses again. As we stood there, people started moving away, encouraging us to place our order, then maybe stand outside and wait. Guess it wasn't only our attire that needed cleaning.

Finally satisfied, I could think more clearly, although a nap was right on my horizon after eating a large pizza all by myself, thank you very much. Jack smiled, knowing all was right in my world again, and we looked for a place to spend the night. The stolen funds were not a lot, but we should have enough to sleep someplace warm and safe.

The next hour was a mash-up of streets and cars, people and smells. Block by block, Jack built up a mental image of the city layout. Fatigue dragged at our heels as dusk moved into twilight. Finally, a small sign on a wrought-iron gate caught his eye, and we looked at each other with a smile.

"The Firefly Hotel."

Perfect.

The delicate pathway, made of river rocks and stones, wound its way through a flower-enrobed garden until the tiny house showed through the branches and ferns. As we entered the creative little building, set back from the business of the street, we marvelled at the solitude of the space, at how no noise penetrated from beyond the front gate. Jack took my hand and gave it a squeeze. If this was an extension of the simulation, maybe more answers would be found here. We approached the desk, marvelling at our surroundings. Every corner, every surface, held wondrous things—treasures from collections only dreamed of. Books and trinkets piled with crystals and herbs. Incense and chimes, flowers of the rarest species. Our hands dropped away, and I turned in awe at the magnificent sights. It was a witch's dream. I released the breath I had forgotten I was holding and inhaled the cleanest air I had ever known, flavoured delicately with a blend of orchids and freesias.

"Welcome!" called a throaty voice. Startled, we whipped around to view our host, hands reaching for our weapons as we moved. Surprise didn't cover it when we realized the word had emanated from a painting on the wall. "Please excuse my absence. We were not expecting you so soon."

"I was not aware we were expected at all!" my mouth spoke before I could think. At the proclamation, both Jack and I had assumed a more aggressive stance, suddenly expecting an ambush. (Though what damage a painting could do was something I had not stopped to think about.)

"My dear, we have known of your arrival on this plain since you crashed through the barrier. It is simply that the two of you deconstructed the challenges much faster than we had planned for. My colleagues had, of course, informed me of your escape from the simulation. Well done, by the way. Rarely do we have humans recognize help from our kind when it is offered."

"You have had other visitors here?" I relaxed and resumed my perusal of the artifacts so casually strewn about.

"In the last millennia, maybe five. We are not listed in 'The Book', you see." The painting twinkled as it laughed at its pronouncement.

"And what book would that be?" I asked, couching the concern in my voice. By now you know I cannot leave a statement like that unchallenged. And with the package we carried, it would not do for them to know about our book too soon.

"Why, 'The Top Sanctuaries in the Universe', of course."

Of course. Why hadn't I thought of that? Faeries. They always think the Universe revolves around them.

I bowed my head. "With deepest apologies. I have been out of touch with the Fae world for many decades. Please accept my humblest and most sincere regrets that your wondrous abode has not been recognized for the fascinating and divine example of magickal wonderment that it is." I learned a long time ago that a little praise pisses them off, but if you heap it on thick, like warm caramel sauce, the Fae are much easier to deal with. Leaning deeper into my bow, I continued: "We are in dire need of your assistance and humbly request sanctuary within these walls and protection from those who would do us harm."

"Thank you, my dear child. Time has been long since we have heard the language well-spoken. Our assistance is granted and we offer you sanctuary." And with that pronouncement, the Fae appeared from every nook and corner. I straightened and looked about with genuine delight as the tiny sparks took identifiable forms, in colours and sizes too varied to describe.

Jack, whose previous dealings with the Fae had gone a tad sideways, stepped to put his back to mine, not convinced that we had not just gotten ourselves into a bigger mess.

"If I may be so bold, where is 'here'?"

"My dearest Stephanie, that answer is not mine to give. Now. It is the time for rest, for food and drink, for fellowship. Come."

The painting faded from view, seeming to shrink into the plaster, while the wall itself thinned and stretched until the space behind was revealed.

A slender, elegant man stood before us, his suit pressed and spotless. I looked down at our dusty attire with chagrin and shrugged.

"If the sir and madam would come this way, I am certain you will find everything you need waiting in your suite." The butler (he was too prim to be a porter) stepped off sharply, and we shuffled along behind, glancing to all sides, awed by the splendour in the small abode.

With the practices gesture of a well-trained assistant, our guide indicated we should enter the open door at the end of the hall. Jack's jaw dropped at the opulence inside, the pearlized walls reflecting the candlelight and enhancing the brightly coloured blossoms cascading from the ceiling. The doors closed softly behind us as we stepped into the suite the Fae had provided. Even I was impressed. It was far more than I had anticipated. We dropped our bags at the door and took off our boots. I wasn't about to mark the pristine white carpet with the debris we tracked through today.

Still stunned by the riot of colours, Jack circled the room, opening doors and touching everything in sight. I understood the need to check its solidity. If I had never experienced such beauty before, I too would want to ensure it was real.

I stripped out of my dusty clothes. Letting them fall on the floor with our bags, I padded across the room in my bare feet. A scrumptious-looking fruit bowl sat on the side table. I avoided it. I may be hungry, but any offering of food or drink comes with a price. Besides, on the top of my list was a shower. Shaking my head at Jack's obvious stupor, I entered the most opulent bathroom I have ever had the pleasure of using. The oaken doors reached to the ceiling, their brass hinges gleaming with the light from the fireplace set in the outer wall.

The ceiling stretched above me like the night sky, open and dark, pinpricks of stars breaking the solid expanse of galactic ebony. Water poured over a rock ledge, forming a natural shower. Gentle ripples moved through the shimmering pool, its sandy bottom ringed with amethyst and garnet. Ivy and hibiscus draped from the stones, ferns and orchids filling every crevice. The aromas mingled into a heady mixture that filled my sinuses and relaxed my tired body. I hesitated to step into the flow, my skin filthy after the days of fighting and running. Jack stepped up behind me and swore.

"Not the reaction our hosts are expecting, I'm sure."

The tension broken, I entered the pool, the warm water lapping at my feet and eliciting a groan of pleasure. Every cell in my body basked in the languid moisture, soaking it in, nourishing me in ways I had not expected. The water was pure, having never contained pollution or chemicals, never touched soap or man-made surfaces. Forgetting where I was, I tipped my head back and allowed drops to slide down my throat. Jack joined me in the cascade, his clothes left in a pile on the floor. His rough fingertips scraped along my back, sending a shiver through my body despite the tropical temperature in the room. Pleasure at his touch, heightened by the warmth and fragrance, pooled in my abdomen and radiated out to spark from my fingers like fireworks. Mist surrounded us as we stood together, our foreheads touching, our bodies slick with moisture.

Hours later, I was woken from my sex-induced slumber by the sound of knocking. Without windows, I could not determine the time of day, my body reluctant to move after our uninterrupted night. Jack lay motionless beside me, oblivious to me stirring or the noise from the door. The fuzzy sensation in my brain slammed home the realization that they had drugged us. Fucking faeries. In my exhausted state, I had been unable to resist the subtle magick that drew us in. As my inner fog thinned, I recalled the shower, the warmth of the water and… dammit. The trail of pits and peels strewn across the floor confirmed my suspicion, and I sighed. What a rookie move.

The knocking resumed, slightly louder and considerably more forceful this time. I groaned as I swung my legs out of bed. Last night's happy muscles protested about being used so soon. Looking about for any article of clothing, I discovered a clean set of leathers. My boots, freshly polished, were waiting for me at the edge of the bed. Fear propelled me to grab everything up and dash to the bathroom. We had been watched last night and our room entered without our knowledge. Jack was going to freak out. I rushed through my morning routine, swiping ineffectually at my mane before storming back out into the suite. I had assured myself of the Book's safety and would confront our host later. For the moment, the messenger in the hall needed to be dealt with.

I flung open the door, ready to attack whoever stood on the other side. The corridor was empty save for a silver plate sitting at my feet. A piece of parchment lay upon it, curled and tied with a gold ribbon. All it was missing was a royal seal, I thought as I bent to pick it up. Wrong. The seal, pressed in wax, was affixed to the bottom of the message.

"Dearest Stephanie. Welcome to the Firefly Hotel. I trust your night was pleasurable." My cheeks flushed, knowing our interlude had not been as private as we might hope. "Your presence is requested in my parlour within the hour."

My face twitched in response to the magick embedded in the fibres. This was an order, not a request. There was much more going on here than I had picked up during our tour. The seal, the image of a dragon intertwined with an ivy and holly branch and wrapped about a planet, was intricate and meaningful to its holder. The wax appeared homemade and dyed in royal purple, its colour bleeding out into the surrounding parchment. Deep in my soul, I felt magick stir. The power possessed by our host was immense. Time to prepare.

I saw no sense in being belligerent. My previous pique at being rousted from our warm bed faded as I puzzled and planned. My enemy was mostly unknown at the moment. Hints from the document told me more than I first believed. To begin with, no male Faerie would use such a delicate emblem. Nor would they endear themselves to me by addressing me so informally. So. Female. Of royal birth, from the presentation and the ancient manner of penmanship and craft. I did, however, allow my human nature to bristle at the directive. Jack remained tangled in the sheets, his snoring deep and rhythmic. He would stay there for hours, if I were to leave him to meet our host—hostess, I amended.

Looking about the room, the shadows deeper with the less-ened candlelight, a niggle of concern pushed me to wake him instead. Not a simple task. Many minutes later, Jack stumbled to the bathroom under direct orders not to step into the waterfall again. Just thinking about the cascade rushed sensations to my groin, the heat a pleasant distraction until he returned. One eyebrow raised as he approached, his new wardrobe hanging from his hands.

"Don't ask," I replied, waving my hand about the room. "Faeries."

His face settled into a mask of annoyance as his glance at the bed showed me he was thinking through all the same thoughts as I had done. I lifted my hand to stop him before he could swear and protest aloud. It would not do to insult them any further. Digging in my bag, I found a piece of paper and a pen, needing to detail my idea before he spoke, either externally or internally.

Scribbling my note as Jack dressed for the day, I handed him my own directions before speaking.

"We have been asked to join our hostess in her parlour," I said, tipping his arm to check the TC for the time. "I believe we will be a bit late, but I am certain she will make time for us." I dropped my eyes to hint that he should read the note before leaving the room, then turned to pick up the parchment.

"My lady," I said out loud. "We would be most honoured to join you and will leave forthwith." Apparently, this was the appropriate response as the paper dissolved into fine, white ash, slipping through my fingers to drift away.

Jack's lip twitched at my phrasing, the formality giving him a better hint as to what, or who, we were about to meet. He tore my note into tiny shreds before burning them in the closest candle. Grabbing up our packs, he looked back over his shoulder before taking my hand in his. This ride was about to get bumpy.

Chess Game with a Master

The majordomo stood poised at the entrance to the parlour, his white-gloved hand holding the door. Within the room stood the most elegant creature I have ever been in the presence of. Her form-fitting gown fell in graceful layers of chiffon and silk, the colours of the skirt bleeding down to form a pastel landscape ring along the bottom. Her power and stature infused the air, and I felt an impulse to curtsy before the princess. Standing in the sphere of royalty has that effect on me. Her very essence screamed 'Bow before me, peasant!' I resisted the pull with trepidation, refusing to show that level of servitude, as I knew Jack would not place himself in such an unprotected position.

Sensing my struggle, Jack inclined his head in acknowledgement of her royal rank. He has heard the tales, stories of encounters gone wrong. Most dealings with the Fae are a tad one-sided, not usually on the side of the human. But then, I suppose, they would look at that differently. Why should they be accepting of humans they do not know personally? We are not the best species in the Universe and are not known for being open-minded. So, as a whole, humans are well down on the ladder of respect that the Fae will give. Individuals have a slim chance of moving up a rung or two if they can prove their worth and their fortitude. While we had found sanctuary here at the Firefly Hotel, it would come at a cost. We can only hope the price does not outweigh the benefit to our cause.

"Join me, children."

The Fae princess appeared to glide towards the small seating area. With a gentle wave of her hand, a china tea set floated down to rest on the table framed by a circle of intricately carved chairs. As we walked forward, the carpet encased our feet like the thickest moss in the deepest forest. Each step brought forth the scent of fallen leaves and autumn flowers, filling our senses with the heady aromas of a forgotten realm. The walls faded from view, leaving a vast panorama that defies description. The colours of the Otherworld are the same, yet different, more vibrant, more deep, just more. It's as if you can feel the colour of everything.

This was not my first exposure to the magnificence of the Fae realm, but it was for Jack. I moved to take his hand, hoping to ground him in my reality. By the look on the face of our hostess, this was not to be allowed. The Fae princess gave a slight twitch of her head and Jack slid out of reach. It was subtle. Jack didn't notice. But right now, he wouldn't notice a two-by-four to the side of the head. Being immersed in the space between spaces is so dramatic that one can become lost trying to make sense of it all. The princess could see my concern for Jack increasing, but he would need to make his own way back. Our communication link was severed. It was more important to keep our telepathic abilities hidden. The best I could do was attach an energetic tether to Jack and hope to lead him back here later, wherever here is.

Acknowledging the power of the Fae, I gave a nod of assent and settled back into my chair with my cup of tea. Last night's lapse was foremost in my mind as I gently stirred the brew, inhaling the citrus aroma. It would be wise to remind myself to never eat or drink anything the Fae 'give' you unless you have earned it. And I had done nothing for her yet. I sat and waited for the questions that were certain to come, now that we were essentially alone in her realm.

"Well done, Witch," the princess gave a small nod. "This is not your first encounter, is it."

Not a question. I waited silently, hoping she would get to the point.

"You have caused an impressive amount of drama on this plain. I hope you have an excellent reason for disrupting our society in such a manner."

Still not a question. I continued to hold my tea, slowly stirring clockwise while my power and intention focused, preparing for the sensory overload I knew was about to hit.

"Let me just take a little look, my dear."

Here it comes. Lesson number two: Never let a Fae into your head unannounced. And definitely, never let them in announced. Bracing myself on the inside, while keeping a smile on the outside, I set my not-so-insignificant barriers to reflect her strength and intention back to her. Even forewarned, my essence took a direct hit of Fae magick as the princess tried to ruffle through my thoughts.

My boundaries fortified, I politely declined her access to my mind and soul, even as my body was screaming for her to get out. Taking in fairie energy is akin to holding onto a high voltage wire and praying you are well-grounded. Gradually, I took control of the onslaught and sent the excess back to the Universe. I could have returned it to the princess, but I was trying to make a point, not an enemy. As the power balanced between us, I prepared my own 'attack'. If I could keep the flow going, I could walk back along her stream of energy and take a peek of my own. Risky business, but one I thought was worth it, if only to show her just what kind of witch sat before her. It would tip my hand a little, but I needed to establish a power base, one that was slightly more equal than she realized.

The princess, her focus more on learning about me than on what was happening, continued trying to force her way into my thoughts and memories. Waves of power washed through me, each one at a different frequency, looking for the sweet spot that I didn't have covered. Fearing she would eventually hit upon the one I used to stay connected to Jack, I increased my response. It was only a slight push back, hoping for a glimpse into the mind of our hostess.

"What are you doing, Witch!"

Looks like she caught on. Here is the danger point. One more nudge, then I retreated without entering her mind. But it had given her a bit of a jolt. Now, I took a sip of tea and pulled my energy back, firmly closing the door to her invasion.

Stymied in her attempt to walk through my recollections, the princess sat back with a huff. Picking up her cup, she sheepishly nodded at the impasse and took a sip of her own. Battle complete.

I broke eye contact to look at Jack, still lost in the overload of colour, his brain trying to sort and catalogue each new interaction. There was little I could do to help. Having been beyond the veil before, I knew that the best way to survive was to muscle through it and Jack would not be satisfied if I were to pull him back to this realm before he finished his assessment. Leaving this job undone plants a longing to return to the Otherworld, to finish that which was left incomplete. We do not have time for that. I could only hope Jack was holding onto his personality and sanity while he created this new log file of information.

Turning back to the princess, I offered to pour more tea before we returned to our discussion. One does need to acquiesce to royalty in some things. Heaven forbid she should pour her own tea after all. And I still need her, more than she needs me. Gently topping up each cup, I broke the silence by apologizing for our presence in her society. It is best to be polite, particularly with the Fae.

"I humbly request your forgiveness for the intrusion and the accompanying upset. We did not foresee the reaction that followed our arrival here, and I sincerely hope that you will accept this apology and be open to providing assistance that we may continue our journey." My brain hurt from stringing so many words together at once.

The princess tipped her head, accepting the words as truth, then looked me straight in the eyes and smiled. Never be fooled into thinking the Fae are pleasant little beings that fly about, leaving fairy dust everywhere. Staring into the eyes of a Fae, especially one so ancient as this, is like trying to navigate the galaxy from a star map. The depths are unfathomable and mesmerizing. Knowing it is an insult to break contact first, I was obliged to maintain my gaze until the princess looked elsewhere. Dropping my shields into place, as this is but phase two of her attempt to gain entry, I left my body to do its job while I mentally barricaded my internal castle.

Her smile faded as she realized this would not work either and that she would have to get her information the old-fashioned way—asking for it. The Fae hate to ask for anything. The simple act of asking puts them in a position of having to reciprocate. I waited to see if she would put herself into that position of obligation, if her curiosity would win over the desire to prevent an imbalance in our 'relationship'.

Score one for the witch.

"Apology accepted." This is an enormous concession. I will take it in the spirit it is offered: resignation.

The princess continued. "Please accept my apologies for

intruding upon your personal space and thoughts. It has been long since I have entertained guests and my manners were not up to standards." More concessions. Score two for the witch.

"Apology accepted." I know a little about the game too. And it costs me nothing to come to her level. "May Jack join us for this discussion?" My turn to concede some ground.

The princess did not want to grant my request. It was flitting across her otherwise stoic facade. Time for another point.

"If there is something delicate you wish to discuss first, I am willing to wait a bit longer." More obligation to me. Which way to go now, princess?

"If it pleases, I would like to talk with you alone first. You are familiar with our ways, as is evidenced by your skilful resistance to my forwardness. May we continue?" Now there is a first. Submission from a Fae princess?? I feel like I have missed a move on the chessboard. Scrambling back through the exchange, I can find no loophole that will leave me on the wrong side of the game.

"With your assurance that Jack will return to me unharmed, and in full capacity, then I accept your terms." Going for broke now. Check.

"You have my word."

Checkmate.

I set down my cup and sat back, content to wait for the princess to continue.

"I am Elarenah, Princess of this realm," our hostess stated, waiting for my acknowledgement of her name and position.

"And I am known as Stephanie DuMonde, Witch of the Old Ways, Protector of Secrets, Ambassador of the Universal Guard." Elarenah's eyes widened. I rarely share my credentials. They make people nervous and dishonest. Not in a bad way, but I prefer people (and faeries) respond to me as I am, not as my title dictates they should behave. But protocol is what it is.

"Does Jack know what you are?" she asked, curiosity making the princess drop the fancy verbiage.

"Some." I acknowledged. "Most." My lips curled into a vague smile. "But not all." It almost pained me to admit that I kept things from Jack. After all these years, there was still no one that knew everything about me. And as much as I had shared with Elarenah, there was more to me than I would ever give to the princess. There is power in knowledge like that, and I was not about to give her the edge.

"I have done you a great disservice, madam. Please excuse my rudeness and the clumsy way in which I attempted to learn details of which I have no business knowing." Elarenah practically bowed with her words, supplicating herself, which is a powerful feeling, but useless to me at the moment.

"You could not know my status and so your error is forgotten. Please think no more of it. Let us enjoy each other's company instead," I paused. "As equals."

The princess pursed her lips at the idea of conceding ground to me, but her options were nil. To refuse me would be an affront to the Universal Guard and the Assembly itself. And while we may be light-years, even timelines apart, the Assembly is far-reaching. A breach such as that would be heard faster than Elarenah could repair the damage.

Sensing the corner she had backed herself into, the princess took a breath, then nodded her assent. Game, set, and match.

"Well played, my dear witch. Well played. You have indeed been invited into Otherworld before."

"I have. I am certain you will check with your brethren upon my departure, but for now, let us work to a mutually beneficial conclusion of our encounter." Now I was stuck in protocol mode. All this talking is tiring.

"Ambassador, how may I be of service?" Elarenah's words were stiff, as was her demeanour. Sigh. It is so much easier to work with beings that like you than it is to work with those that feel they have to.

Here goes nothing.

"We have been tasked with the protection and delivery of a particular tome of knowledge that is, as yet, still encoded. Jack is my confidante and a Knight of the Guard, having defended me in many battles and across many plains of existence. Our enemies mean to use the book's contents to do great harm to any who do not ascribe to their way of life. It is these beings who have wrought so much destruction upon your world. They are known as the Ferin, the attack dogs of the Gretorian Council. I offer my apology for leading them to your door. I am not in control of where the Universe sends me, as the Book dictates where the next piece of my puzzle may be found."

As the princess digested what I had shared, I sent a mental shake to Jack, sending him a lighted path to follow back to me. He had been lost for long enough.

"These Ferin. What is their mission?" Straight to the point of the problem.

"They wish to gain possession of the Book and stop me from deciphering its pages. Ultimately, their plan is to use the power within it to control the Universe," I paused dramatically. "And to kill me."

Elarenah arched one beautifully crafted eyebrow and leaned back in her chair.

"There is much for us to discuss, my dear," she said as she set her tea aside. "Let me tell you a tale…."

Fae History

"In a galaxy, far, far away," she began with a pensive smile, "many wondrous beings co-existed and acted as caretakers for the wealth of knowledge, gathered and kept for millennia as a record of all that is known in the Universe."

"Over time, a faction developed with a singular directive: to limit access to our libraries to those who had shown an advanced mental capacity, to create a divide within the races based on intellect and skill. The 'Haves' and 'Have-Nots'. It was subtle at first, little more than the suggestion that beings such as the Fae and Angels were better suited to being knowledge keepers than humans. Whispers spoken in public venues, rumours spread, inferring that humans were less than capable. As you well know, beings, no matter their race, want to belong. And so the divide grew, with the Fae and what are now the Otherworld beings distancing themselves from humans and other 'simplified' races. We did so out of a misguided belief that we were protecting the Universe and its knowledge in the best way we knew how. Much of this, you already know." Elarenah's speech reflected her first-hand experience, giving proof of her reign as a princess. As immortal as I have become, she is truly older than I will ever live to be, having seen so much more than I could ever hope to witness. And some I am glad I have missed. Though I find myself puzzled at her assumptions regarding my knowledge of Fae history.

"Our egos led us in the ever-widening disruption to our society, which had existed peacefully for eons, years beyond our counting. Some blamed the Angels, some the Fae, some the other races. The humans, having been excluded from the discussion as being 'incapable of understanding', began an uprising, claiming their rights to the knowledge they had been a part of collecting and cataloguing alongside the rest of us." Elarenah fell silent, lost in the remembrance of days lived many millennia in the past.

"This all took time, you must understand. Centuries, in fact. Time enough for some factions to siphon off knowledge, to keep secrets where there had been none. Distrust became the norm, with everyone segregating themselves to their species. Believing that only their own could be trusted, seen with, or allowed within the Halls of Wisdom. It was a period of great unrest and dishonesty. What had been a collaborative society, filled with light and goodness, had degenerated into a cesspool of tyranny and power-hungry beings who sought to hold all things to themselves."

Elarenah met my eyes as she continued. "I cannot excuse the actions of my brethren, of the Angels, of the Otherworld beings who played a role in the War of Eden. In the end, we are all a part of each other, nothing more than reflections of the good and bad we see within our companions and our enemies. I have spent many centuries looking back to where it all went wrong, how we got pulled so far from our utopia. We had everything. We shared everything. And then we didn't. In the luxury of hindsight, it looks like it happened overnight. When you are in the middle of the subterfuge, the innuendo, the subtle mind-games, you can't see the big picture. We all lost sight of the big picture." Elarenah stopped as she struggled to put into words what the war had been like. "In the end, each race or species went its own way, some with a connection remaining to the Universal Truth, some with no knowledge of where they came from, of what they had lost. The battle was gruesome to be in, with so many losing so much."

Elarenah fell silent, grieving for loved ones, for the damage caused, and for what could have been. She seemed smaller as she sat there, overwhelmed by the cascade of memories. My heart ached, the grief feeling very real, the images like scenes from my own past.

'Psst. Steph.'

Jack's back! I tried not to let the relief show on my face. I monitored Elarenah, watching for signs that she was returning to this realm. A quick wave of energy to Jack was all I could manage before the princess shook off the silver webs of recollection and took a sip of her now tepid tea. The china cup rattled in the saucer, her hands betraying the heartbreaking emotion, the flood of feelings she had relived for more years than humans can imagine.

"My family had been one of those targeted as subversive. We did not believe in the divide, in the separation of the races. We believed there was no need to limit access to anything the Universe provided. How could we make that decision? It was not up to us to say who was capable and who was not." Elarenah sighed, filling the surrounding space with the heaviness of regret and loss.

A thick cloud settled around us. Elarenah could no longer speak the words to express what she had lived through. Instead, her thoughts projected themselves onto the misty air and formed a memory-movie of a life long since lost.

Bits and pieces appeared and faded, snippets of faces, beautiful buildings and elegant cities. Artwork and paintings, rooms full of books and scrolls, graceful staircases, shining wood and gleaming metals. The knowledge of a multitude of lifetimes, of treasures unimaginable. The best of the Universe, collected and openly displayed. People and beings of all races, colours, shapes and sizes, coexisting within a vast community. There was peace and harmony… and then there wasn't. The scene morphed into the darkened era of persecution and abandonment. Through her memory, I watched the vision of a Universal gathering place, a society of all, crumble and fall away, leaving chaos and ruin in its stead. . Unable to bear the destruction any longer, and unwilling to change their beliefs, Elarenah's family fled, taking with them all they had learned and only what they could carry.

Choosing to exist as they wished, those who believed as her family did, scattered themselves among the stars, creating a psychic security field wherever they landed. Hiding in plain sight, or living behind the illusions they were forced to adopt, the outcast Otherworld beings became legendary in their existence. Myths and stories, some based in truth, many in mistruths, created the barrier behind which the Fae and the others lived out their centuries, always scanning for signs of compatibility in those who crossed their path.

As the image blurred and faded into the ether, I sensed Elarenah's energy waning. Her shoulders slumped as she shrank into herself. She was so tired. Eons had passed since she had been home, been within the comforts of other Fae, supported by the structure that vanished in the Uprising. While she and others of her kind made a place for themselves, the encroaching populations threatened even these bastions of sanctuary, making the Fae wary and weary of the nonstop projection necessary to protect their very being.

Jack also sensed the change in her and advanced his awakening. While the celestial slide show swirled around us, he gathered his strength. Having some experience with the Fae, Jack knew he had one shot at freeing himself from Elarenah's influence. Leaving him to complete the process, I turned my attention back to our hostess.

Setting her cold tea aside, she released a sigh that held the emotion of forty lifetimes. I heard within it the distress and fatigue of endeavouring to be a leader and protector for her people while simultaneously trying to find other Fae. Explaining our journey and our mission may be just what our reluctant hostess needed to hear, to receive confirmation that she is not alone, that other members of Otherworld continue to survive following the expulsion from their homeland.

Her next words let me know she was thinking along the same lines.

"As you are well versed in the expectations and courtesies of our culture, you have evidently been in the presence of others such as myself. The knowledge would not be found in any tome that humans would have normally been privy to. Not to mention the language barrier." Her eyes glistened with unshed tears, not a single drop daring to track down her flawless face.

She stood and picked up the tray. "I would have some fresh tea brought to us, but I believe you would like a moment with your 'human' partner." Elarenah turned on her heel and vanished into the illusion of the parlour we had started in.

I pursed my lips as my mind raced. Dealing with the Fae is always a delicate dance, and somewhere in the past few minutes, I had allowed her to read my emotions about Jack, probably when I anchored his energy to mine. Nothing to do about it now. That damage was done. The implication that we were not human, at least not in the most fundamental sense, made me pause. By birth, I was. Or understood myself to be. Looking deeply, I found vague recollections of a woman I believed to be my mother, but the longer I lived, the less the memories held up. I had no accurate memory of my father, nor my brothers and sisters. Yet I knew they were there at one time, in the time before the shipwreck, in the time before some deep-seated mutation was activated.

The walls flickered with a display of my own thoughts. A young girl appeared, suddenly ripped from her life, packed off on a voyage to a strange country. Destiny placed me upon that doomed vessel. I was the reason my family perished in the freezing waters off the coast of Canada. They would not have been there if it were not for The Madam's damned quest and my curiosity. I volunteered to make the voyage for her, believing I owed her that much for all she provided for me and my family.

Briefly, I saw my father standing on the deck, looking forward to a new land with more opportunity and less restriction. My mother, who wanted little more than a break from the tedium of her life. My siblings, all but my eldest brother, had boarded the ship and immediately it became their playground. The enthusiasm of youth brightened the walls, their laughter faintly ringing, and my heart tugged at the memory. And there I was. Excited to travel to a new country and work through clues on my own. I was naïve enough to believe it would be easy. The Madame and I had worked through so many of them together that I held firm to my belief that I would have no problems. My naïveté was shattered when our ship wrecked in the night and nearly all of us perished beneath the uncaring waves of the Atlantic Ocean. The scene was so real as to make me shiver, the cold sinking deep into my bones.

A shift then from the ebony darkness of a forgotten beach to a litany of faces, of strange women and lonely men. Alone and destitute in an unfamiliar country, I learned to steal, to hunt, and to please men. This is not as hard a choice as it may seem. Being reasonably pretty, men would buy me things, give me places to sleep, keep me in fine clothing. But the women shunned me, sometimes with cause. Their looks like daggers still showed in the memories as they cascaded into the floor.

Faster and faster, the images fell around me. I could not hear the voices now, but the words were etched in my heart. Sorcière, rougaroo, witch. And I had to believe them, for I did not age as those around me did. The strong wooden walls of my cabin appeared, bringing with them the feeling of loneliness as I kept my distance from the town and its people, choosing to lose myself in the wilds of the countryside. Being declared a witch became a self-fulfilling prophecy. The more people cast me aside, the more time I spent honing the skills I needed to survive, learning natural remedies, being lost in thought. And if that made me a witch, so be it. Baskets of herbs and bottles of elixirs lined the shelves of my home. I was searching for an answer no one could give.

All these recollections flickered across the walls. Snippets of time, like pieces of newsprint, scattering in the wind. I watched as gathering townsfolk repeatedly drove me from my home, their fear evident in the light of their torches. From the distance of time came glimpses of battles won, of new places and old hurts. Through it all, my face seemed much the same, despite the turning of the clock.

The images Elarenah had shared triggered more than simple emotion within me. Mixed in with my own remembrances were fleeting scenes and fragments of memories similar, but different, from what I had lived. Their patina suggested an earlier time, one which I did not yet understand. An uneasy feeling picked at my brain, as though a thought lingered just out of reach.

"So, witch. Are you going to explain your true presence to me? Or shall I take another try at finding out in my own manner?" Elarenah had returned with a new pot of tea and another cup. Knowing she had most likely witnessed my inadvertently projected mind-movie, I shot her a steely look that made her sit back in her chair, a slight blush rising on her cheeks.

"I beg your forgiveness. I have overstepped myself again. It has been long since I have had company and have forgotten my manners." Elarenah dropped her gaze.

"Let that be the last breach," I stated with firmness, the space between us crackling with tension. "I am calling Jack forth to join us, as you obviously anticipated, since you have provided a cup for him. Please pour him some tea so it can cool as he returns to my side."

Expressing her displeasure at being reduced to the position of a servant, Elarenah hesitantly complied with my request before sitting back and inclining her head in a brief nod of concession.

Tugging on the energetic tether, I sensed Jack shake off the last of the Fae influence. I turned back to Elarenah, sitting back and settling into place with my hands free, choosing not to drink anything further. It may be nothing more than practical suspicion, but I just didn't trust our reluctant princess to stay out of my head.

"Jack. We are ready for you when you get your bearings."

While I spoke that out loud, I sent a silent message at the same time.

'Don't drink or eat anything. Or make eye contact. Come in and stand behind me.' Knowing Jack, he would take the instructions with his usual masculine twist, slightly annoyed that I thought he needed to be told what to do. I could only hope he would listen long enough to assess what he was walking into.

'On my way, my dear. Anything else I should know?'

I tried to keep my face neutral, but the sarcastic tone made the corner of my mouth twitch in an unexpressed smile.

Elarenah's eyes widened as she felt the energy flow between us. Maybe our mind-speak was not as quiet or as secret as I had hoped. Or maybe the look on my face was giving me away. It is so hard to carry on two conversations at the same time. Jack makes it look so easy. Regrouping, I turn my focus back to the princess.

"Tell me more about your life here, about how you created such an elaborate scenario. There are so many layers. How much do the inhabitants know about the space beyond? Surely you must have some people who are more curious, more adventurous. Do they all have accidents in the forest? Simply vanish? Humans are an investigative species. Your illusions will not dissuade them all." Thinking back to the people we had interacted with, the doctors, the police, the hotel manager, all just living their lives, I saw the simplicity of the world built on this planet. She and her kind had brought humans with her, allowing them to live in their bubble, observed by Elarenah but not influenced by the Fae. The illusion held as Fae magick blurred the edges, dissuading anyone who became too curious. As the population grew, the illusion would move back. If the populace overgrew its space, Elarenah could generate a catastrophe to reduce the numbers. Superstition would limit exploration into areas the Fae were protecting, like the man-eating forest.

Elarenah smiled. She set her cup down as Jack entered the space and placed his left hand on my shoulder. As the princess raised her eyes to meet Jack's, I rested one hand on top of his, lifting my face to him as he leaned down to kiss me, preventing Elarenah from gazing upon his face.

"So sorry to have missed the party. I was unavoidably delayed." Jack stepped back from me, gradually pulling his hand from beneath my own. Crossing over to address our hostess, Jack bowed before picking up his tea. Raising it to his nose, he sniffed the aroma subtly rising from the china. "Forgive my forwardness, your highness, but I am a suspicious man. I would hate to be reduced to a drooling puddle in the corner while you two ladies continue your conversation."

A knowing smile curled my lips, while Elarenah blushed, caught in yet another attempt to influence us into being controlled. Jack moved his seat so he could see beyond me, protecting my back as always. With my security in place, I raised my eyes to meet Elarenah's. Not showing any fear, I smiled at her and let my mask slip just a little. I have found it often speeds up the process to instill a measure of respect in your target. And I have heard more than once that I can scare the crap out of people if I turn my mind to it. The Fae are harder to intimidate but by no means impervious to a little magick themselves.

Elarenah's pallor lightened several shades as a small portion of my hidden nature showed itself. Jack has seen my not-so-human face a few times, but even he started as I briefly revealed a fragment of my hidden side. Personally, I have not seen my reflection, or know if it would actually appear in a mirror. There are many stories about vampires and other magickal creatures. My intention today was merely to set the playing field, make it a bit more even.

Elarenah swallowed delicately, setting her cup down with a nervous clatter, sitting back primly in her winged chair. She took some time to settle, wrapping her energy tight about her like a cloak. Jack stifled a grin, knowing full well how rattled she had been. It appeared I had made my point with the princess, even while giving a few secrets away. Time would tell if I had revealed too much. Distracted, Elarenah lost focus as she sat and thought about what I had shown her.

"Now that all of our cards are on the table, shall we talk like equals and put the posturing on hold?" I morphed my features back into place. With a small smile on my lips, I sent out my aura, pushing against the field Elarenah had created, adjusting the view about us to be of the Earth we had travelled from. Slowly, the space around us became a deep deciduous forest, filled with the sounds of birds and the smell of moss and dampness.

Elarenah looked about as her illusion vanished beneath my own. Her eyes dropped, and she fell to her knees, the fight draining out of her as she hit the floor, bowing before me.

"I beg your forgiveness, Ambassador DuMonde. I owe you my life."

"I have no need of your life, Elarenah, only your help." I bent to lift the ancient fairy to her feet. "We are here to gather something important to our mission, something important to the Universe. Our job is to collect the information and be on our way. We need a place to hide from the Ferin. I ask your forgiveness for the destruction our presence has brought to your world, and for the chaos that will ensue until we have departed."

Elarenah wavered, concern marring her features as she processed my statement. Jack helped the princess back to her chair before returning to stand behind me, more for support than security, as nothing could penetrate the illusion I had created. For the moment, we were lost to all who passed by, including her own people.

"If you tell me what you need, I would be honoured to locate it and bring it to you," Elarenah offered. "How can I be of service?"

"To be honest, we have not had a spare minute to find out what we are looking for."

Elarenah looked back and forth between us, surprise register-ing. "How can you find a thing that you know nothing about? How can I help you if you know not what you need?"

"What we need is a room without a view, food and drink that is not tampered with, and the ability to search your records for the information we seek. We need access to your library and to any relevant documents stored here. There would have been a beacon that drew us, though we are not privileged enough to know what the sign was. Was there an occurrence in the days before our arrival that came to your attention, something that feels ancient?" Describing how we find our relics is harder than I thought. Usually, we just wander around and find sources on our own, like an archive or newspaper office. This Universal scavenger hunt without rules is hard enough for us to live through without trying to explain it.

Elarenah's face became closed and her voice took on a new quality, one of interest that also held a slight hint of smugness. "Your needs shall be met. With faith in your honour, that upon your word, no harm shall come to those within our walls, we grant you sanctuary. And I will inquire about any sign that may aid in your search." Elarenah sent a mental message to her staff. At least she tried. Leaving my barriers in place any longer would be an insult. My illusion dissolved and in its place stood the old-fashioned parlour. Elarenah nodded elegantly in my direction as she relayed the request to the other Fae, calming them, reassuring them she was fine and in good health. I inclined my head a mere inch, no more, accepting her hospitality.

This was a risky point, as her subjects could mass against us and it would take more than just my magick to repel them. Elarenah likely knew this, but protocol would dictate she honour our agreement. Having the word of a Fae, provided they are the right words, is a significant testament to their concession. They will never break an oath, but they will take advantage of any loophole you might leave them.

Elarenah stood as a figure appeared in the doorway. Raising to our feet, Jack and I turned to watch the entering Fae. She bore a striking resemblance to our hostess.

"Mother, I have prepared the room as you requested for our guests." Turning to face us, the young lady motioned for us to follow her back into the hotel.

"After you," Jack gestured Elarenah to step ahead of us, leaving her no choice but to lead the way. Following the princess, we stepped back into reality and the solidity of the real world. The lobby reappeared before us, and we returned from the space between. Shaking off the clinging sensation of crossing through the veil, I reached for Jack's hand, needing just the small measure of comfort found in contact with my beloved.

His composure remained strong, despite all he had witnessed. A gentle squeeze of my hand affirmed that he was not running scared. Even after the glimpse into the realm beyond our seeing, he had held on to his sanity. The influence of Elarenah's visions may have battered him, but his mind was still his own.

Following our two fairies through yet another maze of elaborately decorated hallways, it was difficult to remain nonplussed by the opulence, to appear as though we saw such wonders every day. All around us hung tapestries adorned with ancient texts in languages not seen on Earth, or most of the Universe, in millennia. The images on the walls came alive with colours too rich to describe, almost unearthly in their appearance, as though they contained stardust. On the floors, rugs of the softest silks and succulent fibres delicately brushed our feet as we passed. Above us, the ceilings depicted the night sky, blending familiar constellations with ones not seen on this side of the Milky Way. Sensing the distractions were overwhelming him, I gripped Jack's hand and pulled his energy into my own, grounding him through me.

'How can you not be drawn in by all of this?' Jack mind-queried, stunned by the colours surrounding us. *'How do you stay so calm, so grounded?'*

'It's not as easy as I am making it look, my love. But I have had more experience with this realm and its inhabitants than you. There is a familiarity for me. Let me guide you from here. Close your eyes, let the colours fade away.'

Jack, trusting me to keep him safe, closed his eyes, keeping his hand in mine and our mind-link open. Elarenah and her daughter lead us past two more ornately carved doors before stopping in front of a new room. Leaning against the portal were our packs, their contents freshly search I am certain.

Backing away from the portal, Elarenah gestured us in. Not entirely trusting our hosts, I sent my aura into the room first, scanning for traps, beings, or spells. As my energy brushed past the young fairy, I heard her suck in her breath with an audible sense of respect and fear. A tremor entered her voice as she bravely announced our arrival and asked if there was anything else we would need that night.

"This will do nicely, thank you." I tipped my head in her direction as I pulled my aura back to me, carefully cloaking the fairies from my energy so that I shared no more secrets this day.

Jack, you can open your eyes. The room is devoid of any creatures or traps I can sense. Can you check for anything I might have missed?'

Responding to my directive, Jack released my hand to pick up our bags before stepping into the chamber to begin his reconnaissance. The door closed softly behind him as I turned back to address the princess.

Settling In

Inwardly I sighed as I sensed an uneasiness, a reluctance to discuss anything further with me. Elarenah stood silently, a guarded look pasted on her face.

"My thanks to you and your household, my lady," I said, hoping to ease the tension.

"Until the morning, Ambassador," Elarenah gave the slightest of bows, her daughter doing the same before they moved off along the hallway, never once looking back. Watching the two of them walk down the dusky corridor, I once again wished for the opportunity to have a child of my own, to bring life where none existed. Unfortunately, life is not a program designed to give us what we want. Exhaling with the pain of a hundred regrets, I opened the door, for the first time laying eyes on the space provided.

The dimly lit room was not at all what I was expecting, given the opulence of the corridors and our previous accommodations. One of these days, I would learn. A room it was. Exactly as I had asked. But it would not win any awards for cleanliness or modern comforts. There being nothing I could do about it,

I cleared a space to drop our bags, disrupting layers of dust that filtered down to the scuffed wooden floor. Definitely no view. I was fairly certain the grime-covered windows were no longer visible from the outside. That suited my request. What I had neglected to include in our discussion was the need for a minimum of tidiness. The basic requirement of a bed with bedding would have been nice. Point to the fairies. I could hardly complain, as I had not been specific.

Jack brushed his hand across the windowsill. He sneezed as his action stirred up the particles that delicately coated every surface. This move in the game went to Elarenah. I let go of my expectations and instead took a deeper look at the room, feeling my way out into the spaces surrounding us. The room itself held no secret passages, no hidden compartments, no bugs (real or high-tech) that I could find. We have stayed in worse places.

Confident we could not be seen, I used a spell to brighten the room. I was not about to give our hostess the satisfaction of asking for anything additional, which would further put me into her debt. The debris collected along the edges before gradually gathering in front of the door. Opening it, I not-so-gently encouraged the pile to scatter itself along the hallway. Beyond the frame, magick made my soul sing. The pulse of a ley line confirmed why Elarenah chose this location for her sanctuary. This room was not connected to a line, but the hallway seemed to run along one. Good to know when I needed to recharge. Feeling my way through the outer edges of the energy field, I probed for information about this world.

From my scan, I gathered we had landed in the largest city on the planet. About the size of the Earth's moon, the signature held little more than the forest we escaped from and the urban area we now hid within. Puzzled at how humans existed for so many millennia in such a small region, I tapped into my Universal guides to source out information about the seeding of the planet. Stretching beyond the small colony, I sensed a large cluster of planets scattered in what we would consider close proximity. The local inhabitants could see the other planets in the night sky.

Having nowhere else to go, I dropped to the floor to think about the past few days.

"Jack? Does your TC still say the year is 4781?"

Jack checked the display and nodded, still pacing about the small room. Apparently finding nothing amiss, he sat with his back to the wall and pulled his recording book from his pack. The face of the device emitted a faint green glow as Jack accessed records and searched the Universal library for any details about where we were, what we were looking for, and how we landed here to begin with. Local information banks would house more details, but this would get him started while we figured out our next move.

Now that I knew who had populated the galaxy, the date made more sense. Humans on Earth count their dates in relation to the death of Jesus the Prophet, using A.D. to separate before and after. This star system never had a Jesus. There was no 'A.D.', just year upon year, lifetime after lifetime. Elarenah started counting when she arrived here and set up shop. The TC was telling us the local time, displayed in a format we were accustomed to. One mystery solved.

Nope, two down. If there was no Jesus, maybe there was no religion that included a Heaven. Without the belief in life after death, spirits wandered about feeling lost, having no place to go following their departure from the land of the living. The little girl who helped us had found passage to the other side of the veil, but so many others seemed to be aimlessly adrift. Thoughts for another time. Right now we had bigger problems.

Elarenah's wards would hold for a day, maybe two. Eventually, the Ferin would run out of places to look, and they would level everything in their path to find where we were hiding. With time not being on our side, and nothing I could do to help Jack, I settled in to gather my strength, reinforce my shielding, and bolster my energy reserves. The fight would be coming to us.

Enter More Mysteries

This damn quest is going to be the death of me. What should have been a simple retrieval of an ancient artifact has become an interstellar scavenger hunt. And the Book is not giving up its secrets casually. The protective spells embedded in the very fibres had kept its true nature concealed for centuries, the clues to its whereabouts hidden in the silted floor of the ocean, lost since the sinking of Atlantis. Then we came along. Working on directives from my Commanding Officer, we had been searching the waters off of the coast of Portugal for many months. Our dive had brought up a small chest, warded against the invading pressure of the sea. And against prying eyes.

This was a treasure so greatly prized, Jack and I left the surrounding seas and set sail for the emptiness of the Atlantic and began our slow cruise of the Earth's many oceans. Staying in motion made for less observation of our studies, and kept Jack busy while I beat my head against the bulkheads, trying to make sense of the imagery so elegantly carved into the chest. While I still cannot fluently read Atlantean, my translation skills are improving. Months of studying and dissecting each tiny detail finally led me to a sigil that glowed when I traced it. Feeling an ancient energy course through me, I carefully followed the carving to a secret latch. With an ear-piercing squeal, the box revealed its contents.

Age and old wine stained the oilskin map. Showing little more than the continents as we know them and a small marker, notes in the legend instructing us to search for the star. So prophetic. And so the hunt began again. Crossing the ocean one more time, Jack docked us in port on Manhattan Island. Our clue: 'It lies within the relics, once lost, twice found.' And this is as helpful as the Book ever is.

I was more than happy to be on dry land. After temporarily depositing our treasure chest in a safe place, we located a hotel to set up in. Jack did reconnaissance for the first few days while I wandered the streets, enjoying the dualistic nature of New York. In a city so large, with so many people, you can be surrounded, and still be alone. There are no simple answers to why I ended up outside the shop that was squeezed into a small alcove on a side street, not two blocks from our hotel. Layers of grime coated the windows, not the least bit attractive to passersby. If my intuition was not so persistent, I would have walked by, too.

Trying not to sneeze as I disturbed the dust surrounding the door, I peered into the shop, my eyes squinting through the gloom to see what lurked in the shadows. While my gut said all was well, my training had me reaching for the knife tucked into my belt, just in case my sensors were malfunctioning. It has been known to happen.

Hidden in the stacks of detritus, I spotted an insignificant man, not much taller than my waist. I struggled to look him in the eye without slouching down. He projected an air of defeat. He could not hide it, though he wished to. The energy within the store was the same. I had seldom felt so much desperation and depression bottled up so tightly, like a curtain that muffled the light from entering. Stepping back to see him better, I stood to my full height and realized that there was indeed a reason for me to enter this melancholy establishment.

Peering beyond the minuscule owner, my gaze fell on a book-shaped pile of dust stacked on a pedestal in the centre of the small store. As I moved past the proprietor, my eye glimpsed a slight shimmer, like that of a firefly. Having caught my eye, I realized it was another defence mechanism. First, the dust, to make it seem unlikely to be valuable, then the fairy to distract anyone not fooled by the camouflage. Upon seeing I was interested in the item shrouded in what appeared to be mainly ashes and cinders, the old man scurried to my side, eager to tell me what he knew about the book hidden under all the filth.

His energy shifted, smelling the possibility of a sale, and he seemed glad to be rid of it. He told me the book had brought him nothing but bad luck since someone had dropped it off in a box of rare collector pieces. Curious, I wiped at the cover and tried to open it. Strangely, the book resisted. Thinking it was damaged, I checked it over, feeling the delicate engravings in the leather and sensing the power it contained but unable to see within it. Perplexed, the owner took it back to show me it was a simple book. Even more curious, the book would open for him, and the pages were blank. He stood in the store, telling me how he had survived a mugging, a break-in, a flood, a lightning strike, and a fire that destroyed everything in a circle around this volume.

I backed away, understanding with a deep knowing how much power lay stored between those two covers. Thinking I would be better off without it, I made my excuses and attempted to leave. I really did. When the Universe wants something to happen, it will. This book was expertly warded against interference. The steps the Universe took to put that book in my path at that time had to be astounding. It was ancient, having been bound centuries before I landed on this plain, yet it appeared in my presence when I would have the skills to unlock its potential without being affected by the destructive abilities it contained.

Now, I am as human as anyone reading this story (almost). And the first time I connected to it, I have to admit the possibilities blossomed like spring flowers. What can't you do with power like that? That's when my conscience kicked in and the Book accepted me as its guardian. Have you ever had a book that you couldn't put down? It was like that, except for the fact that I really couldn't put it down. In the parsecs it took for me to adjust from 'Oh how fantastic!' to 'Oh how dangerous!!', the Book bound itself to me. When I said earlier that we kept a close eye on it, that it was never far from our grasp? Yeah....

I have often wondered why the Universe did not simply wink the damned Book out of existence. Over time, I have learned that Energy doesn't work that way. There needs to be an equal and opposite reaction, and destroying so much magick in one place, at one time, would be cataclysmic. Black-hole type of destruction.

The author had bound the Book in such a way that only someone as dedicated as I, would work through all the protection spells and puzzles to safely reveal the information contained within it. Not to mention there are not a lot of almost-immortal humans wandering this planet. One lifetime would not be enough to unravel the secrets. Thus, the Book needed me.

And, as it turns out, I need the Book. For hidden in its pages may also be the secret to my longevity and possibly an antidote. You might think living forever is a gift. Not when you are living it alone. For now, I have Jack. But if we could return to a normal pace of life, I think I would like it. The grass is always greener, isn't it….

Several hours later, Jack woke me out of a much-needed nap.

"Stephanie, can you bring out the Book for a minute? I hate to ask, but I might have found something, and it's the only way to know for sure."

Knowing he would not have asked if he wasn't on the trail of something important, I began the challenge of removing it. Experience has taught us to keep it close at hand. Running from bad guys doesn't leave us time to fetch it from some secret hiding place. In a state of desperation, I had created an internal place for the Book to reside, hidden from prying eyes and sticky fingers. Being a magickal tome, it didn't actually exist within me, but it didn't exist outside of my body either. It sort of hovered between dimensions, only becoming solid when I needed to use it. It's complicated. To trigger the process, I envisioned the Book resting in my hands. There was a peculiar sensation in the area beside my stomach, as though something was preventing my insides from moving into the hollow left by the Book's exit. It was not a small object, yet when hidden, I had no conscious feeling of its existence within my abdomen.

With a shimmer, the Book gathered together and grew dense, coalescing into a tome bound in leather and tooled with symbols neither of us understood. As I turned it over in my hands, images carved into the cover glowed, subtly at first, barely changing the surface colour, yet compelling me to pay attention as the messages played across the carvings. Setting it down, I pulled out my notebook and pen to scribble down the shining symbols as they spun in a dance. The changes came faster and faster until it appeared as though the leather itself would catch fire. It was magickal to watch, but hard to keep track of. The sequence repeated until I recorded everything the Book would share. The light display slowed down, eventually fading away, leaving an imprint on my eyes as I re-read my scrawled record.

I tilted my head back and forth as I tried to make sense of my writing.

"Well, it's either trying to tell us we are close to the clue we are seeking, or that the Book wanted some fresh air. It has been tucked away for a while."

A tiny smile creased his lips before Jack returned to the TC, looks of puzzlement crossing his face as he deciphered the information on the screen. I turned my attention back to the string of symbols written in my notebook, comparing it to documentation from our past encounters.

"These still remind me of the Egyptian hieroglyphs —"

"There are other kinds?!?" Jack interjected with a big grin.

"Wiseass," I smirked in response. "Maybe there are, and we just haven't found them. Better still, maybe their images came from a book like this one, some ancient text not yet rediscovered on Earth."

Jack considered the idea for a moment, then shook his head as though he had enough to think about without pondering the methods of communication in the time before time.

Staying on my Egyptian/Ancient alien theme, I continued my dialogue. "OK. Say there is another text, another relic from the library that made its way to Earth, the same way this one did. Only it was found sooner. Or maybe the Fae at the time were friendly with the inhabitants and shared their knowledge, at least enough so that not everything was lost." My mind raced ahead, picturing multiple scenarios—the sunken city of Atlantis, the library of Alexandria, wonders built with technology humans have not advanced to. How much had been destroyed? How many more discoveries were still waiting to be found? More visions drifted through my mind, their vividness remaining as the images faded. I shook my head and turned back to the task at hand, leaving more mysteries for another day.

Tracing my finger along the sequence the Book had shown me, I felt the magick beneath the cover pulse and travel the path of my fingertip. The magick intensified, adding to the glow of the book, and an unfamiliar pattern emerged. Following my intuition, I traced the pattern again and asked the depiction to reveal itself to me, bringing it to life above the text that held it. I slowly turned the Book beneath the hazy form that hovered in the air, willing the image to hold its shape.

Jack lifted his head and stared at the spectre, his jaw dropping when he realized that I had discovered something new. From my vantage point, I could not see the entire picture, but Jack could. I must have turned it in just the right way for him to witness the portal the image created, a glimpse into a vast celestial system.

"Stop! Hold it right there! Let me get a better look!" Jack cried, as animated as I have ever seen him. He grabbed his notebook, frantically scrawling pages of notes, drawing images of things I could not see from my side of the holograph.

"WHOA! There's a whole other galaxy, maybe another universe. What the hell have we got here!?!"

Jack's handwriting degraded to the spastic markings of a crazed squirrel for all the sense I could make of them. I sure hoped they would spark some recollection for him once he pulled himself back out of the image and into this reality. As I impatiently waited for Jack to record as many details as he could, I found my mind drifting off on a journey of its own. Willing my body to remain upright, I allowed my consciousness to follow the trail of breadcrumbs the image had given me, seeking responses to questions yet to be asked.

Questions like: What the hell is going on? How did I get into this mess? Where the fuck are we? Life-altering queries I could mull about for hours and get nowhere simply because the answers are not to be found.

As for this quest, every time I think I have a grasp on the puzzle, someone changes the picture and drops the open box on the floor. Searching through those pieces now, I resisted the desire to right things and really looked at them where they lay. Like cards from a Tarot deck, there were hints, each image as intricate as a delicate snowflake, with more details revealed when you looked closer. Delving deeper into my mind, I let the bits settle around me, shifting, revealing hidden parts, hiding others that may or may not be of any use at the moment. All intuitive work is like that. There is wisdom in everything we see, it is all in the interpretation. But what I saw made little sense.

Physically aware, I can feel the patina of the wood beneath my legs. The ages past have left their imprint on the structure itself. The dusty air of a room, long-unused, brushes against my nose. Dried branches rustle along the roof, or perhaps a critter is making its way across the shingles. The energy of the Book weighs heavily on my lap, almost pulsing as it also waits for Jack.

'Turn the Book, Stephanie.'

I heard Jack in my mind. Strange. Why wouldn't he just say something? He can tell I'm not sleeping. I picked up a level of urgency in his voice. As I open my eyes and turn my hands to look for myself, Jack suddenly yells, "Wait! I'm not done yet!!!"

WTF? Shaking my head, I stop and hold it steady as Jack returns to his scribbling.

'Disconnect, Steph. You have to let go.' Jack's voice, again, in my head.

'What do you mean, disconnect? Disconnect from what? I'm not touching anything?'

'The Book! Stephanie, drop the Book!!' Jack sounds frantic now, not at all the cool cucumber he usually is.

"Why are you in my head?" I asked out loud. "Why don't you just say what you need?"

The Jack before me looks up from his notes, startled by my proclamation. And in that instant, I could see something else. Something not Jack. Something not right.

I scrambled to my feet, pulling our treasure in close and

backing up as fast as I could to put distance between me and the impostor sitting on the floor. With too many questions and not enough time to get answers, I wrapped myself in magick, sealing the Book within its secret pocket as I back-pedalled for the door. Which was no longer there.

Sigh…

Bring It

Facing the very real person before me (and I use the term loosely), I rolled my shoulders. All of our training better be good enough. The tension in the room ramped up as 'Jack' casually rose to his feet and shook himself. Oh, goodie. Where were my magick skills hiding? How had they cloaked someone with Jack's energy and mannerisms so supremely that I missed all the clues? Elarenah would not be happy to see me when I finished mopping the floor with her little surprise. Assuming I survived, that is.

'Jack? If you are not in here with me, where are you exactly??' I mind-messaged my partner, hoping to hear he was just outside the door, waiting to be invited in.

'I would love to be able to tell you but....'

I shifted my position, never taking my eyes or my attention from the impostor before me. *'Elarenah is not going to be happy. I might need some backup in here. If you can find me.'*

No help coming from that angle. And the shape-shifter before me was altering himself in subtle little ways. If I had not been watching, I would have missed the slight lengthening of his arms, the extension in the fingers, not to mention the claws starting to show. Now that the jig was up, the werewolf sped up the process. As the being stretched to its full height, I heard the muscle tissue being pulled and the bones settling into new positions. What once sat before me in human form would soon be unrecognizable, and close to unbeatable. My right hand reached for the scar on my upper left shoulder, my body subconsciously recalling the battle I had barely survived. In a bit of a hurry, I tried to hit the highlights of my last encounter, hoping my experience would be enough to prepare me for this go-around. Instead, it scared the crap out of me and I shook my head to send the memories back into the vault.

What I had learned the first time was to interrupt the transformation. My best chance at an impactful strike would be near the spine and neck, preferably before the face gained all its teeth. Narrow window, narrow room. Limited options. As I circled around and searched for a weapon, I glanced at the notebook 'Jack' had been using. Bingo! Watching the rapidly changing werewolf, I tried moving to my right, hoping it distracted him enough to let me slide by. His head snapped in my direction, his shifted eyes boring into mine with all the intensity a predator can project. But my motion arrested his change, and he could not maintain eye contact for long if he was to finish the shift. Taking advantage of the slimmest of blinks, I dove for the discarded pen, sliding across the floor and slamming into the wall on the far side of the room. The werewolf spun and roared in anger, his transformation nearly complete, his towering form filling the room and pushing me to the brink of panic. There was simply no room to move where he could not reach me in seconds.

Sensing the same thing, the were stood before me and glared, his eyes the tawny gold of a wolf with a tinge of the brown they had been before. The beast-man leaned down to stare me in the face, his energy giving off the confidence that this battle was already won, so what's the rush. He intended to play with his food. And he did. I scrambled. He smacked me with a fist the size of a bowling ball. I hit whatever he threw me at. Knowing I would not last much longer in a physical fight, I needed to change the game.

I allowed my shoulders to droop, gradually hanging my head and closing my eyes, giving the appearance I was accepting my fate. The risk that the werewolf would lunge forward and break my neck was an enormous risk. But I had no chance of survival if I tried to meet him at his full height. And I did not have the stamina to inflict the amount of damage necessary to win this fight. So I centred myself, gingerly exposing the back of my neck, willing the were to take the bait while praying for the speed and strength to see this through.

The room filled with the sound of the beast breathing. Fear rippled through me as I tapped into his primal hunting instinct so near the surface I could taste the blood he was anticipating. That seemed a little creepy since it was my blood he salivated over. Matching my inhalations to his, I crept my hands and elbows into the position I would be counting on to save my life.

My fingers wrapped around the only weapon in the room,

Jack's pen. I angled the tip to make the best use of the point in what I hoped was the most vulnerable spot on a werewolf. This is all guesswork. There is no credible data in the archives about werewolves and how to slay them, and if there is, I never considered the information relevant. I mean, really, how often is one expecting to bump into a werewolf? Note to self: Everything is relevant. Just because you have never seen one before does not make it imaginary. After all my years and all my training, I still screw things up. Hoping that one shape-shifter is much like another, I set myself, and let go of everything but where I was, and where the were was.

As I mused about the very verifiable existence of the creature looming over me, the depth of my predatory roommate's breathing changed. It was almost subtle enough for me to miss, and I would have done, had I not mated our inhalations earlier. Bringing myself back to focus on the disaster lurking before me, I released the link and inhaled deeply as I prepared for the onslaught. Oxygen flooded my muscles, preparing to react in the one instant I had to reach my mark.

Mistaking my full exhale for a sigh of regret and capitulation, the were tensed his legs and his knuckles cracked as he flexed his paws. Trying not to become nauseated by the dripping saliva pooling on the floorboards, I listened for the intake of breath that would signal the imminent attack.

The timing was so crucial I could not attempt to guide my weapon to its end goal. I needed to trust that all the training and muscle memory would generate the required outcome. With the slightest of exhalations, the were surged forwards, all of his focus on the tasty section of spine I had shown him for bait. The gaping mouth grazed my head, and I curled my shoulder under my body to roll onto it. As my body changed angle, I used the stored up energy to thrust the pen deep into the exposed throat of the man/wolf as his impetus propelled him past my position and left him without a target.

The small room added its measure of damage, the werewolf colliding with the wall before he could arrest his motion. Ignoring the 'weapon' lodged in the side of its neck, the creature shook off the impact and turned its cold eyes my way once more. While the were righted himself, I backed into the farthest corner, scrambling for any other item I could use to defend myself. This next piece would not be so easy. With nothing else at my disposal, my only option was going to be a frontal assault intending to pull the pen back out of the were's throat and use it again.

Sighing dramatically, I shifted my feet and adopted a more hostile stance, signalling to the werewolf that playtime was over. The man/wolf huffed. I think he was laughing at me. As he straightened up, I watched the slightest trickle of blood ooze through the fur of his neck. Thinking for a second, another option popped up. What kind of witch am I, forgetting to use magick when in a fight with a supernatural creature? Giving myself some slack since I hadn't had a breath in which to think of anything except survival, I now let my mind work its way through the collection of spells gathered in the past century, searching for one in particular.

Carefully circling to the left, I tried to draw the were into a little dance, hoping to get a better look at where I had wedged the pen. The shifter merely stood there, still quietly huffing. Now I know he's laughing at me. Apparently, I have become the main course and the evening's entertainment. Time for a different distraction.

"Well, I definitely was not expecting to deal with the likes of you today. Or any day, to be honest. I just have a few questions: Do you rip up all your clothes when you change? I mean, do you do it that way every time? 'Cause, that would leave you naked somewhere every time you changed back. Great skills in the makeup department. You looked like Jack—excellent likeness, by the way. You had me fooled and I know Jack about as well as anyone—but in your everyday life I bet look like someone fairly average. Today you got to be someone spectacular looking. Was that a nice change for you? Being the most handsome man in the room? I imagine it is hard enough being overlooked by the ladies just because you don't stand out in a crowd, but then there is this whole 'I become a wolf once a month' thing. That has got to be tough to explain. It's hardly fair. I mean, women get to have 'off days', why not guys? Right?"

Jack has always been patient with my chatter, but I know I can be an annoyance. This is where I am hoping to use this skill to its maximum potential.

"And what about your diet? Can you eat in restaurants if they serve steak tartar? Does the smell of raw meat make you agitated, invoke your primal instincts? That can't be easy on a first date. Assuming, of course, you can even 'man' up

154

enough to ask someone out for dinner. Maybe you are the dine-in kind. I'll bet that's it. Online dating and internet chat rooms. Do you ever get out of the house for social events that don't involve other weres? Are there other weres? You aren't an orphan, are you?? That would be awful. I mean, I'm an orphan, so I totally get the 'I don't have any family' dilemma. Sometimes it is a benefit, you know. No one to answer to if you stay out late. Who's going to give you shit for leaving fur on the floor? How do you exist in the everyday, mundane world? Do you have a job? I bet you do security in some enormous warehouse where you can't talk to anybody, like, ever."

Rambling and rapid-fire questions have two effects. First, your target gets slightly confused trying to keep up with the train of the conversation. Second, they become annoyed, and then pissed off, mostly because it's wasting their time. The result is most often the same, and I don't care how I push them to that point. When people (or werewolves) get pissed off, they drop their guard for an instant, usually only long enough to roll their eyes. And that was the instant I had been looking for.

The whole time I was chattering, my mind was searching for a particular spell I read sometime in the past five or six decades. My mouth continued spitting out random questions, and although I would have liked to know some of the answers, I was not about to stop aggravating the werewolf long enough to hear one. Pushing harder on each little nerve, I simultaneously moved my body to keep my hands out of view as I began the motions that would activate the spell. Sensing the were was near the tipping point, I shifted gears and showed him my empty hands. Like any talented magician, tricks are our best-kept secrets and the best protection of those secrets is misdirection. Thrusting my hands out, palms facing him in the classic 'Look, they're empty' fashion, the shape-shifter glanced at them out of sheer habit. In that split-second, I shouted the incantation my brain had finally located in the filing cabinet I call a mind.

"Illustrium inflegre!"

The were looked at me, mildly curious about why I felt the need to yell as if I could scare him away with a sudden loud noise. What he missed was the spell driven from my outstretched hands and aimed at the one entrance into the were left unprotected—the pen in his neck.

I dove to the floor, curling myself to shield as much as possible from what I hoped would be my saving grace, with emphasis on it working before the shifter ripped me to shreds. In that awful half-second, I heard the werewolf chuckle and inhale as he reared up to strike my exposed back.

"WHHOOOSH!!!"

I held on tight to my knees and made myself small, praying that the inferno building inside the werewolf would remain contained. At least, that was my intention. But I am still human — sort of. Curiosity got the better of my good judgment.

Peeking up from my huddled position, I saw a drop of saliva splash to the floor just as the were returned his focus to me. There was no time to scream or rethink my choices today. As I hurriedly tried to retreat into the wall and breathed in what I believed would be my last breath, as the werewolf's front teeth grazed my cheek, there was a pause in his momentum. A puzzled look replaced the predatory gleam that had been inches from me the moment before.

Standing to his full height, the creature desperately began clawing at his own throat. In that instant, it realized I was not the one about to die in this tiny room. I scrambled to the closest corner, grabbing for anything that might shield me from the flying debris the shifter was about to become. The wolf became frantic and, realizing this may be his end, turned back to me, the hatred showing clearly as he took the two steps necessary to bring me back into his reach. He had no intention of going out of this world alone. Raising his massive paw, the shifter arced his arm back and began the movement that could smash me through the wall I was cowering against, and probably through the next one, too. The animosity rolled off him in waves I could see. As the emotional storm slammed into me, I struggled to breathe, the weight of his fixation impeding my lungs, making me weak and vulnerable. This shifter was so much more than your average predator. A magician and practitioner in his own right, my opponent switched gears and tried to stop the impending inferno, but his transition from attack to protect came too late.

I slumped to the floor as the last of my oxygen petered out and

I approached the blackout point. Focusing the remnants of my thoughts into a protective spell, I warded the book against all comers, hoping my last act would at least keep this knowledge out of the hands of whoever found my body.

My last memory before my eyes drifted shut was a large, hairy snout breathing into my face, then nothing. Just nothing.

Damage Report

"I missed it! DAMN IT!!"

As I regained consciousness, I ignored my physical state. Injuries heal, but experiences, once missed, can never be repeated. I slammed my fist into the floor beside my head, still curled up in the corner I had sought refuge in.

"Ouch."

With a groan, I gingerly rolled onto my knees and hands, slowly pushing my badly bruised body into a semi-seated position. Noting the small protests (and larger screams) from the battered muscles and scraped flesh, I made a mental note to avoid fights with werewolves for the foreseeable future. I am fairly certain I entered this room with unblemished skin over most of my body. The few tattoos I sported were subdued compared to the brilliant blues and purples that profusely peppered me now.

Taking as deep a breath as I could manage, I assessed the reliability of my major muscle groups. Feeling an unpleasant strain in my right knee, I shifted onto my other leg. And the world went dark…

"Ouch." Now this feels familiar. Thinking back through the haze, I took stock of my injuries while steeping in the puddle pooling around me, seeing as how the last try at moving didn't go so well.

And speaking of puddles, what exactly was I laying in? Deciding that my injuries weren't going anywhere, my brain turned to the analysis of the muck surrounding my location. I watched as it seeped into the dried floorboards, oozing and creeping its way into the minuscule cracks and crevices. Note number one: The slime was still in motion, so I had not been napping for very long. Number two: The coloured goo was not blood. Specifically, not my blood, making it a safe assumption the mess I was lounging in came from the remains of the shape-shifter who had been locked in here with me. By Elarenah. We were going to have a little chat, the princess and I. But that was a pleasure for another time. Onto number three: The wards of the room offered protection against magickal penetration. I could use only what came in with me. Access to the ley line beyond the now-hidden door had been terminated.

Since I was not leaking my fluids all over the floor, I assumed I would not expire from my injuries, as numerous as they were. Now for the fun part. What did I break this time and how badly. Recalling I passed out the last time I put pressure on my left side, I made what I thought was a smart decision for the moment and left those parts alone. Scanning from my head to my feet seemed like a logical progression, something I could do with little movement to avoid bringing about another fainting spell.

Being a bit of a chicken, I opted to focus on my right half, skirting into the left if the area appeared to be battered, but not broken. Basically, my body believed it had been pushed through a meat grinder and pulverized. A shape-shifter had slammed around me. Injuries are to be expected. My upper back had withstood my impact with the wall and sliding across the floor. From what I could tell, mostly bruises with a smattering of splinters for good measure. Not so lucky in the rib department. Breathing deeply would be an issue until I set the two cracked ones back in place — again. I continued my scan internally, and I seemed to have protected my organs well enough.

Now for the lower half of my body. Steeling myself against the potentially incapacitating pain, I cautiously searched for the source of my previous crippling reaction. My right side shows nothing detrimental that a week on a white sand beach couldn't cure. Now for the left side: thigh, knee, ankle — uh oh. Broken or dislocated. Damn it. And now that I have acknowledged it, nothing else matters. All the rest of the bumps and scrapes faded into the background as the damaged tissue roared to life and demanded attention. I think I was better off passed out.

Fatigue would be my biggest enemy now, other than my injuries. I had not eaten well in days. Healing requires energy, and I was running on empty. Gathering what little strength remained, and being careful not to knock my left ankle against the floor, I started dragging myself to where the door used to be. It was a slow and laborious process, and the slime didn't help. Bits of fur, gunk, and what I guessed were bone fragments clung to my skin as I inched my tired body closer to the inside wall of the fairy domicile. At least it was an inner wall when I entered it. Hanging my head for a moment, I realized I forgot to ensure I was even going in the right direction.

I had a decision to make. Use the last of my energy to reach the door and potential escape, or scan first and risk not getting there at all. Survival above all else. It's a powerful motivator. Risking more fairy trickery, I resumed my arduous journey to the door. I would only need a smattering of energy and magick when I reached the frame, just enough to force the door to open. My last hope for a long life hinged on the warding only being in place within this room, this magickian trap.

And Jack. Somewhere on the other side of that door was the love of my life, possibly in the fight of his life. Or a fight for his life. And I would not let him fight that battle alone, damaged ankle or not. My survival may well depend on him being on the other side of this damn door. But I couldn't see what waited for me, couldn't sense it either.

As I made the slow progression across the remaining floor-boards, I worked on forming a protection spell to hide behind once I popped the lock. Two spells at once would drain the last of my stored magick. I needed to reach the ley line on the other side.

My crawl towards the door was agonizingly slow. As my

energy reserves depleted, and I called upon every ounce of strength, I felt myself begin the slip into unconsciousness. Even a witch can only support life for so long. Limited food, the lack of drug-less sleep, and the fight with the werewolf had all played a part in the fatigue that threatened to overwhelm me. The subtle call to sleep, just for a moment, tugged at my body. An urge to lay my head down on the worn floorboards, to embrace the coolness of the old wood, began a slow petition to my injuries and beckoned my mind to let go.

Warning bells chimed in the last corners of my brain. Struggling to open my eyes again, I spotted the barest shimmer of the magick I had brushed up against as I crept towards the only exit.

A sleep spell.

Seriously.

Fucking faeries.

On one hand, I grudgingly had to admit that they had almost won. Only my years of training saved me this time. With arms and shoulders filled with energetic lead, I resumed my journey, pushing past the stickiness of the ward, only then considering that there was likely a fail-safe trigger embedded in the spell. I have now warned the faeries. One of us is leaving this room. And since they were expecting the shifter to win the fight, they probably created the ward to allow his safe passage. Or maybe he was a pet, kept tamed by warding like this placed throughout the building. I pinned my hopes on the latter. I no longer had the energy to maintain my protection spell. This was my last chance to breach the barrier between my captivity and my escape.

Reaching beyond the shimmer into the reality of the room, my fingertips made the briefest contact with the wall where the door should be before it was flung open, throwing me to the side with its momentum.

"Stephanie! Oh My God!!" I felt Jack's body land on the floor next to mine.

"Stephanie, can you hear me?!"

My hero…..

My Hero

As I began the groggy shift from the realm of the unconscious to that of an actual living person, my brain began the slow realization of three things: one — I am not dead after all. Two — I am out of the room. And three — Jack had come to my rescue one more time. It is really hard to be the heroine of your own story when the other characters keep stealing your thunder. But, since I would most certainly have died this time if it weren't for Jack's timely arrival, I was going to give him this one.

"Jack??" I softly queried. "Are we safe?"

"For now." I sensed Jack sweep the area, back and forth, back and forth. Satisfied we were well hidden, Jack took in the damage to my body, focusing on the one part I hoped not to touch. A bit of a coward, I tried to tuck my damaged ankle out of view. It needed to be mended for us to have any hope of getting out of this disaster, but I was not looking forward to the method it would take to put the bones back where they belonged. Jack took my face in his hands, tenderly kissed my split lip, then moved his hands down my leg. I couldn't tell you what happened next. I'm sure you can guess.

Several minutes (maybe hours) later, I attempted to sit up and open my eyes. Unprepared for the swimming sensation, I sank back down to the floor, feeling decidedly ill. It was of little comfort that I had nothing to throw up. My stomach would try anyway if I continued to rush my recovery. Resigning myself to playing the damsel in distress for a little longer, I swallowed the bile which hung in the back of my throat and asked Jack for an update from my 'fainting couch'.

"Do you remember when you told me not to trust the Fae? That appearances mean nothing? And how I laughed about it? 'How dangerous can such a little thing be?'" Jack asked rhetorically.

I nodded, immediately regretting my action as the world spun in multiple directions. "Yes, I seem to recall those conversations." I squeaked out, testing my damaged throat and ranking it a seven on the 'good to go' scale.

"Stow the sarcasm, Steph. I mean, really. Why would I believe the stories? They are always shown as being delicate and glittery. Who can distrust that?"

I unsuccessfully attempted to arch one eyebrow as Jack continued to justify his errors in judgment. I ruefully shook my head, quickly closing my eyes against the vertigo swirling through my brain.

"Okay. So the sweetness of that girl swayed me. I forgot she has had centuries to perfect her innocent appearance. And Mommy dearest can sure pour on the charm. My head swam with all the attention and the promises." Jack paused for a minute and took my hand. I risked opening my eyes a crack to see him sitting with his head bowed.

"I almost lost you." The whisper held his fear and grief, and I watched a single tear slip down his cheek before he raised his head to look at me. I opened my eyes as far as I could, banishing any thought of being sick. The swelling kept me from fully completing the action, but the anguish on his face broke my heart.

Crying should be therapeutic. Cathartic. Not the way I do it. My version is ugly and noisy, and nowhere near the delicate 'damsel in distress' I was emulating as I lay in Jack's arms. All the stress and frustration, the hurt and anger, the betrayal and the fear came gushing out in great sobs and torrents of tears. I do not know where my body found so much liquid. Jack's shirt became streaked with the salty water mixed with dirt and all other manner of gunk from the werewolf. Despite that, he held me tight, letting me release all the emotions vaulted deep within me for so long. Too long, apparently. As our tears mingled, a whiff of something familiar reached me. It was only a hint upon the air, but my witchy brain latched on as if it were the safety bar on an amusement ride and I was about to plunge down a cliff.

Magick!

Hesitating to break the moment, but realizing that I had moved through it already, I slowed my breathing to match Jack's, deliberately creating our strongest bond. As our exhalations fell into a rhythm, so too did our heartbeats. Jack sniffled, then realized what I was doing. I gently reached one finger up to his lips to silence his question before he spoke. I spooled in the magick, gorging on it like a shipwrecked sailor seeing food for the first time in weeks. The quantity made me realize how very little reserve remained after my ordeal, how depleted my stores were. I don't think I could have made it out the door if Jack had not burst in the way he did. But I didn't know that then, did I? We can do so much when we haven't been told that we can't.

I have found no greater 'high' than magick. It fills the spaces between, well, between everything. If there is room for oxygen or blood, there is room for magick. If there is space for thought and memory, there is space for magick. And my body drank it up, enough to replenish my aura and little else. But it was enough. Inhaling deeply, sending the magick throughout my body, I dropped my head back to Jack's chest and sighed, temporarily content knowing that I would be okay. And if I could make it, so could Jack. Faith and hope are powerful things. Moving past the point of despair to that of belief makes all the difference. And, at that moment, I believed we could survive anything.

Jack kissed the top of my head, the gentlest of touches, filled with every word that stuck in his throat. I nestled in closer, unable to say the words either. Instead, we blended our auras, letting their energies swirl and mingle, sharing silently but in a manner so powerful it was like watching the birth of a star.

Drawn to the magick we were creating, the tiniest sliver of the ley line came within reach. It was powerful, overflowing its banks, saturating the area that we had marked with protection sigils. Magick unbound by ritual or practice, elemental and raw, completed the boundaries and erected walls of energy so forceful I was almost begging a Fae to touch it. I just wanted to see a tiny puff of smoke, not like a display of fireworks or anything.

Sharing my wish with Jack, he chuckled. "Can I make a wish too?" he asked. "Can I wish for Elarenah's magick to be reversed? I'd like to watch her run around her own house for a while, trying to find a way out."

Both of us laughed at the image of the elegant Elarenah stomping her dainty little foot when her wards refused to obey or her china teapot stopped brewing her favourite blend. There are definitely much worse things we could wish on an enemy, but those are things we like to dish out in person. And that time would come soon enough.

Feeling safe again, I drifted into a dreamless state. My body had a lot of healing to do and I prefer to be unconscious when I have bones to mend and bruises to soften. Jack slipped to the floor beside me, and we slept, cocooned together in our bubble of serenity, trusting our wards to hold all comers at bay.

Taking Stock

"Just five more minutes…" I groaned as Jack stirred beside me. I was still groggy as he sat up and stroked my back. I curled into his hand, relishing its roughness on my sensitive skin. Sighing, I stretched and moaned as the flood of injuries took turns in the lead as they raced their complaints back to my brain. As I took stock of which ones were crying the loudest, it pleased me to discover that, while I was far from recovered, the biggest complainer was my stomach. I believe the statement involved my throat and whether or not it had been cut. This was apparently the only valid reason for not filling its request. Priorities.

Jack rolled onto his back, stretching out the kinks and muscle knots collected during our nap on the floor.

"I don't suppose you packed food on your way to my rescue," I asked with a slight pout, still trying out the damsel persona.

Jack looked at me with a straight face, then heaved himself to his feet, reaching out a hand to pull me to mine.

"Guess not." I stared down at my stomach. "Sorry, man. One

more day won't hurt us—much."

Rolling my shoulders to release the stiffness, I checked for any intrusion while we slept. Rats! Looks like we missed the smoke show. I wonder who touched it. Guess we'll find out during our departure. Someone should be missing a finger or two. Putting weight on my injured ankle. I have to give credit to Jack's medical skills. While it was tender, the wrapping job gave it enough stability that I should be able to move reasonably well. Time would tell if it held up.

A grin met my gaze as Jack handed me a canteen from his bag. Trust the soldier to be prepared. Doubt pulled at me and the question showed in my eyes.

"Don't worry. I filled it at the pizza place while you were begging for change. Yours is full too if you haven't lost it." I would be dead without this man. My head gets so stuffed with magick and 'woo woo' that practical things, like life-saving water, never seem to get my attention.

The water was warm and tinny but I didn't care. It could have held five-year-old water and I still would have drunk it. Sounds close to ecstasy rose from my throat as I licked my lips. Jack shook his head. The simplest things can make my day.

I tucked the canteen back in his pack. Time to step out into the faeries' domain. We moved through a few exercises to clear the last of the cobwebs and limber up as much as possible. Spooling up some energy for the road, I packed in as much magickal juice as my battered body would hold. Beside me, I sensed Jack making mental and physical preparations for the fight we both knew was waiting around the corner. Looking beyond our wards, through the shimmer that magick leaves in the air, I made out the shape of a door and a window, a room much the same as the one I had battled the werewolf in.

Having a basic layout of the room to work from, I constructed an exit strategy, choosing to share my thoughts with Jack through mind-speak as I sensed advancing energetic forms outside our barrier.

'Jack, we have company. Numbers unknown.' I scanned the area beyond the door and took a glimpse out of the window, but saw nothing from that portal.

'You take point. I'll cover our rear.'

'My thought is to pull the door open and send an image into the hallway, maybe provoke a response, see what we are dealing with out there. Make sense?' I crept to the door, my fingers brushing the handle when Jack tapped my hip. Freezing in place, arm outstretched, I stopped and waited for his assessment.

'Back up slowly. Don't turn your head.'

Trying not to panic, I did as Jack directed. What had I missed?

'DOWN!'

I hit the floor in response to his 'verbal' command. Above me, the door exploded with the impact of a well-placed energetic shot. Oh, goodie. A faerie sniper. Now they know we both survived. And we know they are playing for keeps. Brushing the shrapnel of wood shavings from my head and shoulders, I peered back along my prone body to see Jack flattened against the floor as well, but scrabbling to find more weapons in the bag he carried. Trying to ride the energy wave back to its creator, I found my search blocked as I probed beyond our wards. Damn faeries.

'What have you got hidden in there, Jack? Anything made of iron??' My breathing slowed down to a more regular pattern, the adrenaline coursing through my body slowly dissipating. My mind had returned to scanning the hallway, seeking the energy signatures I had hit on before they had made the assassination attempt. All had gone quiet. The faeries had either backed out of range or cloaked themselves in the moments of distraction. Sigh. I am not on my game today.

In the meantime, Jack had gone through his entire pack, finding nothing to help in this situation. It was likely that the sniper was waiting patiently for our next attempt at leaving the room. They could hide in the space beyond the door, or move to another spot with access to this room, making their stand in a yet-to-be-discovered location. Keeping our heads low and out of our enemy's line of sight through the window, we moved back to the centre of the room, drawing our energy around us in a tight circle, reinforcing our wards.

Reaching beyond our position, I tried to grab the ley line tendril I had tapped into previously. Nothing. We were stranded in this room, with little to work with beyond our training and skills. So here goes everything.

Jack slithered along the floor, stopping every few feet and reaching up to tap the wall, searching for an alternate egress. This could also be the entry point of any gathering attack force. Leaving the physical world to Jack's capable skill set, I moved into a realm I was comfortable in, the realm beyond our seeing, where all things exist and all can be known. My ability to step into the Universal plain was the reason they had selected me to be a Guard, what had gotten us into this mess in the first place. Now it had better get us out.

Stronger than I was yesterday, I put my physical body on hold and 'checked out', as Jack calls it.

"You should warn a person before you do that," Jack sent through the veil. "Do you have any idea how much that freaks me out?!" I looked back to observe my body slumped on the floor, devoid of all signs of life. Even my breathing was almost non-existent. At a glance, I appeared dead. That part always got me, too.

I blew him a kiss that Jack felt shiver across his cheek, his hand reaching up to touch the skin as though to hold on to the sensation.

"I'll protect you with my life, my love. Come back quickly. We have little time."

His circle of the room, finding no obvious hollow spots or

panels, Jack assumed a posture that kept the door and window in full view, while keeping my prone, helpless form protected from attackers. Knowing my back was quite literally covered, I entered the realm of the Etheric beings and stepped into the space between spaces.

The feeling of being outside of my body was liberating, yet scary. I resisted the urge to look back again, set my shoulders and moved through the wards. The moment of truth. If my magick was as strong as I believed it to be, the Fae would not detect my presence. I would feel successful if the reconnaissance generated nothing more than a glance in my direction. Remembering that the Fae are ancient elemental beings in their own right, I kept my distance from any area I felt they might be in, choosing instead to look for a path we could use to reach the hotel lobby, the centre of the Fae's power structure. I considered navigating to Elarenah's inner sanctum and finding a treasure she valued above all else. It might give us the leverage we needed to force this encounter to a positive conclusion.

Moving as swiftly as possible without causing ripples in the earthly air, I marked the corners and walls with energetic 'breadcrumbs' to assist in our departure, anchor points my magick could grasp as we travelled to keep us on the right path. Trying to guess what tricks the Fae would incorporate in their attempts to keep us trapped in their world would drive me all kinds of crazy. My energy would be put to better use finding us that special something to give us an edge.

The hallway narrowed and turned, heading off in split directions, curling back on itself, offering no straight path to follow. The labyrinth threatened to make me lose my mental bearings until I divided my spirit energy. Leaving one half at ground level, the other lifted, changing my point of view to scan the hotel from above the rooftop. The solid portions of the building became hazy and less concrete, the open areas having a gentle glow as I moved through each section. Moving rapidly so I did not deplete my energy before I reached my destination, I risked discovery in order to get to my target. The longer it took, the greater the potential of injury to my inert body. And to Jack, who was diligently covering my six.

I slid along the walls as I came close to the hiding places of the Fae. Leaving a marker at each location to warn me on my return, I scanned the bodies within the rooms as I passed, looking for our hostess. Noting the absence of Elarenah, I scoped out where she might wait for me, hoping she would not expect my energetic foray into her personal space. While Elarenah had tried to determine just what kind of witch I was, I don't think she probed in quite the right way. The potential breach was Jack. Under the influence of her daughter, and possibly the princess herself, I had no way of knowing what he may have unintentionally shared. My prime focus shifted to not getting killed while I was walking around skinless. Death in the Etheric realm is a very real death, your energy dispersing among the stars, with galaxies between particles. One does not easily return from that.

Moving beyond the tangled hallways and into the main building structure, I rejoined my spirit halves and walked the floors, certain that the key force of the Fae protectorate was waiting for us to make the first move.

A subtle melody lilting on the fringe of my range of hearing drifted through the lobby. If I strained, I could almost make out the words, at least enough to understand they were not English or any other language I have learned in this lifetime. Fae. And probably not good for me to focus on. Or was it? The song strengthened, building upon itself as more voices joined in, creating a symphony so beautiful it would make you cry — unless you were me. Not in physical form, no tears. And now I knew where they were and what their tactic was. Humans are fragile creatures, prone to many foibles, one being emotion. The presentation of that emotion is what gets us killed. If the Fae made us feel grief or sorrow, the gut-wrenching loss of loved ones, the sheer weight would take us out of the game. Torrents of tears streaming down my cheeks make it difficult to focus on my target.

My last marker planted, I retreated through the dusky spaces, noting each twist and turn to create a mental map of our route. Hoping I was strong enough to come back to life, and that Jack remained alone in our tiny room, I raced back as quickly as my ethereal form would allow. It's difficult holding all your particles together by sheer will. As I neared our hideaway, there was an awareness of dread as a rivulet of fresh blood wended its way under the door. And the engulfing silence. Sickened at the thought of what waited for me, I steeled myself for the carnage I sensed lay just beyond the simple plank of wood.

Recovery Mode

Jack's heaving back, blood dripping down to pool around his feet, was a welcome sight if you are into that kind of thing. At this moment, it was perfect. I slipped through the door expecting a war zone. I got that. In spades. The Fae had sent some big fighters; the bodies stacked up according to weight. Some of them would rival professional football players. The tiniest like children in our eyes, small and dainty, looking every bit the fairy princess they might have been in life. The battle had been fierce, and Jack had not come through unscathed. Some of the blood might be his, but until we could wash the rest from his skin, it would be impossible to tell the damage he sustained while standing guard over my 'corpse'.

When his head lifted, two bloodshot eyes met mine in an eerie connective moment that showed me the depths of his worry. Sweat dribbled down the side of his neck, stained to pinkish hues, darkening as it ran towards his torso. Through the patchwork of bruises, I saw bite marks and cuts, some deep and potentially painful. The bites concerned me, as I could not see any animals in the pile. Hoping they had not brought in more shape-shifters to bolster their numbers, I crossed the room towards my body, still feeling the intensity of Jack's watchful gaze, and returned to the human form still lying inertly beneath his guard.

All this time, I was not really dead. My heart continued to beat, my lungs to breathe, though each functioned so shallowly as to appear deceased. It was my consciousness, my essence, that took a little stroll through our hostile hostel. Now came the challenge of reintegrating my 'soul' without disrupting the rhythms which kept me alive. My heart beat in a slow, steady rhythm and I matched my shadow lungs to the pattern of my chest rising and lowering. When my exhalations synchronized, I counted the breaths. One. Two. On 'three', I snapped my energy back into its well-worn places, hoping I had gotten all the bits at the same time.

Taking an off-balance breath, I pulled the air in to feed each cell, bathing in the increased oxygen as the energies blended, the spiritual with the physical. Above my prone form, I could hear Jack's heart, still pounding with the adrenaline aftermath of the battle he had waged. Consciousness returned to my brain, and with it, my connection to Jack. Relief coursed through him as the realization that I had survived entered his fight-fogged mind. Tension eased from his shoulders as he stepped back to give me room to move and stretch. My concern for Jack's condition almost outweighed my need for a few more vital minutes to fully reintegrate. This is not a process to be rushed, but my heart screamed for answers, my brain racing with possibilities. It is difficult to watch your loved ones when they are suffering and be helpless to do anything. It would be mere moments to wait as my body regained itself, but the anguish written on Jack's face made it hard to resist forcing the transition.

Jack fell to one knee beside me, sensing the debate I was in. We have been here before. We know how this works, but each time is still different. Jack reached out to brush the hair from my face and the time-roughened tips of his fingers contacted my skin. Inhaling the scent of the man I loved, my mind raced through our past encounters, touching briefly on the highlights of our time together. Each moment came back to this—the slightest of touches, tender and sweet, connecting all of our being to one another. It is more binding than any contract, any vow.

Heaving in a deep breath, I immediately regretted the choice. This was not a room you wanted to inhale in. The scent of copper hung around us. Unable to withstand the oppressive odour of decay any longer, Jack coughed to clear his airways. The violent expulsion of air carried with it a spray of his own blood. One of those wounds must be deeper than it appeared. Fear for his life propelled me to move faster, recover quicker, rush the process. I would not lose him. Not this time. Not again.

As Jack knelt on the floor, his energy faltering, I sought the injury that was robbing him of his life. Jack tried to still my fingers as they frantically moved over his torso, his skin sticky with a mixture of blood and gore no forensic team could ever analyze. I realized tears were tracking their way down my cheeks, adding to the genetic mystery coating us both. This isn't fair. Not after all we have been through, all we have fought through. Not with our end goal finally within reach. This fucking quest. If it cost me Jack, I would tear the Assembly apart with my bare hands. I am not going to do this shit on my own, not anymore.

Jack's face slackened as the blood loss affected his body's capacity and function. If I didn't stop the bleeding, I would lose him. And should he die, Elarenah is not prepared for the level of wrath that will follow. Revenge was a dream best left to simmer while I performed more magick. First, I needed to find the damaged blood vessel or internal organ. The spray suggested a lung puncture. Hoping I guessed accurately, I sent a beam of healing light into Jack's body as he began a slow slide to the floor.

Hours passed as we sat together. My healing energy was depleted, my magick as well, but Jack's chest rose and fell in a ragged pattern. As his colour slowly crept back to a shade less closely resembling death warmed over, I released my embrace and allowed my shoulders to relax. Collapsing from the strain of it all, I slid to the floor beside him, placing his head upon my chest as if it were a pillow. And I slept.

Showdown

"Not that I don't enjoy where I am, but don't you think you could have chosen a better time and place, Steph?"

My sleep-drugged brain struggled to make sense of Jack's statement. Apparently, his strength was returning. Good. It might have been tricky to crack that pretty little face of Elarenah's all by myself. I would have done it. But having a partner is a benefit when battling Fae of her stature and age.

Fingers delicately walked themselves over my body. The tingle I felt with each caress fed the fire I sensed in him. Decades together meant the simplest touch was enough to make us forget the world even existed, to make us get lost in one another. I swallowed the sob threatening to escape my throat when I remembered how close Jack had come to dying mere hours ago. Tears formed in my eyes as the feelings of loss surged, on the verge of spilling over. Sitting up, I gripped my face as if I could hold in all of my emotions at the same time.

"Shh. Don't cry, babe. It's okay. I made it." Jack's touch turned from desire to compassion, a delicate motion that allowed me to release the torrent of feelings so tightly held within my heart. The overwhelming flood of tears, the mental and physical strain of the past few days, the energetic toll the whole mess had wrought. It was finally too much. I don't know how I will get the salt stains out of the leather. Time ticked away as the waterworks flowed. Knowing I must look like a waif from the streets of some ancient, dirt-covered world, I endeavoured to wrap up my pity party. I swiped the grit and grime from my face, replacing it with a different layer of particles, most of unknown origin. Jack gently wiped the last stray droplets from my cheeks, then he gave me a kiss that filled the hollows of my soul, erasing all the fear and worry.

Leaning his forehead on mine, Jack held my face in his hands, his thumbs lightly caressing my skin. And I just breathed. I breathed in the air he exhaled, taking in his essence. I breathed in the knowledge that we had survived another night on this god-forsaken journey. And I breathed in the certainty that when we reached the end of this escapade, someone somewhere was going to come up with more suitable answers. Enough with risking our lives for some damn quest that no one ever explains. I. Was. Done.

Jack lifted his head. Our eyes met briefly, and I wondered what he saw in them before he straightened up and sat back. He tipped his head as though he wanted to ask a question, then simply grinned.

"Shall we?" Jack asked as he helped me to my feet.

Stepping over the pile of dust the Fae had turned into

overnight, we approached the door, falling back into our standard attack formation. The years of practice made it so effortless, no signal or thought passing between us as we flanked the door and yanked it open to expose the hallway.

The empty hallway.

Well, that was anti-climactic. They might have left one guard outside, somebody for us to fight. I didn't believe Jack had killed them all the day before. I know I heard beings in other parts of the building when I had been on my walk-about. Today the silence was total. Not even a hint of activity. We shared a glance before stepping out of the room. The ley line lay beneath our feet. Tapping into it, I pulled in the magick. As I allowed the energy to fill my every cell, I simultaneously sent feelers back out to search for any information about our current situation.

Nothing.

There was just nothing.

That, by itself, did not reassure me. I would much rather be certain where my enemy is than play hide-and-seek. And with the destruction of her home and family at our hands, Elarenah is most definitely going to view us as the enemy. Oh, goodie.

Making sure we left nothing behind, we took one last look around us and walked down the hall, following the markers placed only yesterday. As we moved away from our sanctuary, a sudden 'pop' reached our ears. Not good. The only thing that sounds like that is magick. Heavy-duty, earth-shattering, sky-bending magick. Glancing over my shoulder, I watched the room and the building begin the crumble, the very ground surrounding our boots doing the same. Shit!

Jack and I raced through the imploding structure. Grabbing onto one another, we scrambled forward, seeking my markers as we ran. We sped through the hotel as fast as possible, each step keeping us just ahead of the cascading dust storm growing behind us. Off to the sides, the effects of the destruction stretched to reach out and pace us. Soon, the only path left was surrounded by a swirling drop into nothingness. The entire building began dissolving. The magick that held it together was dwindling. Elarenah had abandoned this part of the hotel and with it went the structure's ability to stay as a cohesive mass. It was not as simple as degrading into dust, however. If this continued beyond what we could see, this planet was about to become a black hole and suck us into some new dimension in space and time.

And me without my spacesuit.

My markers contained enough magick to anchor segments of the hotel in our current reality. Everything else deteriorated into particles of matter. Soon we would be standing in the lobby that no longer existed, possibly on a planet that also ceased to be.

We made the last turn towards the entrance and skidded to a halt. I knew the Fae would not leave things undone. There they stood. At the end of the hallway. The last of the guard entrenched behind the ley line magick they used to hide their presence. Their shielding was strong, as was their intent. It projected loud and clear. We shall not pass. Between them and us lay a small mound of tattered clothing and a tarnished sword. Bending down to touch the delicate skin, her warmth filled me with joy. A survivor. I rolled the body over to reveal the face of the one Fae life worth keeping. The one that would guarantee us safe passage.

I looked over my shoulder, hoping to see how much of our path still stood. Without the walls and other parts of the building in the way, the remains of the corridor showed briefly through the clouds of debris filling the surrounding space before being devoured by the maelstrom. No escape there. Turning back to the greeting party, I took a stance over the prone form of the young princess and prepared for yet one more battle.

Ace in the Hole

History does repeat itself, doesn't it? Why do I keep ending up in situations where everything turns to dust? Brushing the grit from my face, I returned my focus to surviving this Fae battle while protecting the Book I have pledged guardianship over. Me and my lofty ideals. And I had to figure out if Elarenah's daughter was strong enough to survive being moved.

Steeling for the upcoming fight, Jack stepped forward. I half-turned to watch the path behind us, searching the swirling clouds of debris for figures hidden in the rising gloom. Energetically, nothing appeared, but that was no certainty. If I could redirect the ley line, disconnect it from its normal flow, maybe we could gain the upper hand.

Not going to be so easy. Elarenah used its energy to create her hotel, her empire, even her world. Now she was using the magick itself to encase it in a protection grid. Any attempt to circumvent the grid would trigger an energetic response. And knowing what might be triggered made me rethink accessing the ley lines myself. I had gotten away with tapping in before, doing little more than alerting Elarenah to our position. This time would have bigger consequences. Think nuclear.

Jack snuck a quick look at me to ask if I had come up with anything. I shrugged one shoulder, then turned to face the Fae army awaiting our advance. We needed a miracle and the best I could hope for was to carry the unconscious princess home. We could not leave her; not when she had fought so hard to survive. She had been so close. Only the shields erected by Elarenah had prevented her from reaching sanctuary and help. That was an oversight she could take up with her mother.

The winds of destruction came ever closer as we looked into each other's eyes once more, embedding the images in our memories, hoping if not totally believing we would meet again on the other side. I pulled off my jacket and dropped it over the child to protect her. In hopes it would not take too much of my reserve, I added a cloaking spell, hoping it would help me find her again. A squeeze of our hands, then into a fighting stance. The Fae shifted as we did, stepping out into a formation that would surround us in minutes if we allowed it. With no option to retreat, we stepped into the fight with nothing more than our fists and a knife or two. I am a much better fighter when I can use magick, but the risk was too high to try, and my energetic battery was empty. As Jack threw the first punch, levelling the Fae at the front of the pack, I stepped into the fray, arms and legs swinging, kicking, lashing out at any body in reach.

The maelstrom reached us as the battle increased. Losing sight of all parties in the choking cloud, I dropped to the ground, trying to see something, anything. Nothing. Dust obscured everything and everyone. And it would soon kill me if I didn't do something to clear my lungs and the air about me. Coughing, I directed a portion of my dwindling magick to cover my head with a dome, extending it only low enough to enclose my chin. Cloying particles lined my mouth and nose as I struggled to breathe. The dome made it easier, but each breath was still laden with dust. I stood hunched over, chest heaving with the effort. Knowing the young princess would be in real danger, I fell to the ground and felt for my jacket. A wisp of leather under my hand and I extended my magick to protect us both. Alarm bells went off in my brain. Jack was in trouble. Reaching out blindly, my fingers brushed against the fabric of his pants. Feeble fragments of my magick flew to his location. A dull thud reached my ears as someone or something hit the ground. Praying it wasn't Jack, I tried to mind-speak, risking discovery by doing so, but frantic to know he was alive.

'Jack?'

'It was not me, angel.' Jack replied. *'Are you okay? Did you find the girl?'* His concern overwhelmed me, as did his voice. Relief flooded through me, taking my focus away from the battle. Not the best state to be in when playing defence. Now that I was paying attention again, there was nothing to pay attention to. The battle noise had stopped. Or at least, nothing was moving in our immediate area.

I reached for Jack, grabbing onto his ankle. He dropped to the ground, enabling me to blend our domes into one umbrella. Crouched together as the storm raged, I laid my head against his chest, happy to inhale in his scent, musk and all. Covered in the ashes of a thousand galaxies, coated with the blood of those who had attacked us, battered and bruised by the beatings we had endured, and all I saw was the most handsome man in the galaxy. My heart swelled at being able to hold on to Jack even for the briefest of moments. For this moment, time stood still. For this moment, we were all that there was.

And like all good moments, someone had to ruin it.

What's the phrase that bad guys always use? Oh, yeah…

"So happy to see you, my pretty!" Oops. Wrong script.

Elarenah's eyes contracted to rigid slits as she approached. Dismay and grief coloured her still delicate features, battling with the outrage that her trap had failed, as had her minions. I half expected her to stomp her little foot and order us to fall upon our own swords.

"You are a tricky one, Stephanie DuMonde, Witch of the Old Ways. You are indeed worthy as an adversary, worthy of your task. But hear this. You have cost me more than you can ever understand." The words formed themselves on the air between us, propelled forward by magick more than breath.

The venom with which she spat the statements sunk deep, gelling into a lump of fear. Elarenah is no newcomer and her power, if fuelled by revenge, will be unstoppable.

"I revoke your sanctuary in this house. In. My. City. My oath prevents me from killing you in the here and now. Do not tarry else I forget myself."

My heart skipped a beat. Partially, in the hope that she meant this encounter was at an end, partly in fear that there would be another one with this ancient Fae. As one, Jack and I stood up from our position and revealed our secret. Still alive, though badly hurt, the young princess had survived the final battle. I stepped back, saying nothing. No words were needed as I watched Elarenah's facade crack with the knowledge she had not lost her child after all. The decision to cloak her remaining army's presence had prevented her from reaching her daughter, from knowing she had survived.

Elarenah extended her hands, and the magick flowed in visible waves as she dropped to the floor to cradle her injured child. Protocol would not allow her to thank us for the grace and mercy we had shown. Her stoic face and a tear of gratitude were all she could show as concern and relief replaced her grief. In my mind, a connection formed, relaying the words she could not say aloud.

"You have acted with honour when I have not. This is a debt which can never be repaid."

The space between us wavered, like smoke curling and floating away. Elarenah faded from view, her daughter's weakened body draped in her arms. This did not make me feel better, as I would rather have eyes on the Fae princess. Hardly daring to breathe, and certainly not prepared to move, I clung to Jack, being content to hold him and draw from his strength.

The storm dissipated. The wind reduced its howl to a more sustainable moan. Jack and I circled the space, stretching for each step before taking it to confirm there was solid ground under the thick blanket of debris. Every motion caused dust to rejoin the breezes, moving ahead of us to settle on the path where we would disturb it again and again as we made our way to the foyer where our 'hostess' had stood.

The darkened sky belied the true time. Not having eaten in what seemed like days, if not weeks, my stomach decided it was time to chime in. Why is this never a thing for action heroes? You never see them stop in the middle of a firefight because they feel peckish. Me? I could stop an entire armoured division with my need to eat. A growl worked its way up, reminding me of the werewolf I had bested. The memory lit up my dirt-caked face, a smile creating cracks in the surface, flakes falling to the ground like the tiniest feathers.

Jack's grin reached me as he shook his head, small mysterious bits circling his body as he did so. We continued to trek forward, feeling like a much-loved cartoon character. Jack tried to whistle as we walked, but his lips would not cooperate. Picking up on his improving mood, I swung our enjoined hands, working my way up to a skip and a hop. Allowing my emotion to infect him too, Jack joined in the skipping and we laughed, the enormity of the experience loosening our inhibitions, releasing our inner child. The tension so tightly wound within us unfurled, our breathing relaxing and more stable.

Reaching the foyer, the dust clouds reduced to puffs on the

breeze we were making with our passing. The faerie guard was gone, as ethereal as their master. Elarenah had departed, but she was a powerful opponent. And while we had done her a great service, I knew we were now marked as enemies of the Realm for the destruction we had caused. Yet one more group that wants my head on a platter. I knew I should be more scared of the prospect, but at the moment, I was too hungry to care.

"I wonder if that pizza place is still open." I pondered, reminiscing about the last good food I had tasted in this oh-so-magical city.

"I wonder if there is a city to get pizza in," was Jack's reply. Always the realist. I pursed my lips at the thought that the city might be gone and I would still not find anything to eat.

Taking one last glance at the room left standing, the actual structure was showing now that magick no longer made it shine. Tired and grey, the hotel office seemed to be decades old, the wood panelling revealing its origin. But if the structure was from the seventies, and the Fae had only recently recreated it in their splendid manner, how did the time on this planet get to be so inflated? My thoughts began the journey down that rabbit hole as we turned our backs on the building and returned to the garden path. The stones stayed firm beneath our feet, the scraping of our toes dragging on the rocks revealing how exhausted we were.

The iron gate creaked ominously as we pulled it back, the paint fading before our eyes. Its elegant veneer vanished as the magick withdrew back to the ley line. We stepped over the threshold. As we did so, the handle disintegrated in Jack's hand; the gate crumbling into a pile of rust and bolts. Brushing the remaining dust from our shoulders, beating our hands against our pants, we resembled two vagrants who had just crawled out of a rat-filled alley.

"Get a job!"

Wow. How rude.

"Don't you know how to wash your hair? Get off the street, ya' bum!"

Jack and I looked at each other, my grin growing. I have experienced the opinions of New Yorkers in the past. If we are truly in the Big Apple, my chances of getting a great slice of pizza just went up.

As rusty as the old iron itself, my mind worked its way around the idea of the gate being a portal. The Fae-created world lay somewhere in the Universe and had been delicately linked to the Earth as we knew it, the gate quite literally an opening between worlds. When Elarenah departed, the deception dimmed, and the portal became closed behind us.

We are back on our home planet. Filthy and tired and oh, so hungry. The noises and scents of New York filled my senses, and I inhaled deeply, filling my sinuses with the heady smells of pollution and melted cheese. Jack zeroed in on a small shop that might not be afraid to take our money.

I lingered outside as Jack went to satisfy my craving. Mainly he did this just so he wouldn't have to listen to me bitch about how famished I am. I slid down a brick pillar, turning my face to the sun. I must have looked like I needed help. Most days I would refuse the handouts, but today, I made seven bucks. Vowing to give the money to a worthy soul, I graciously accepted their coins, giving each donor a gift of healing in return. Being a witch has some benefits.

Jack returned with my pizza and tossed me a bottle of water. We moved off to a small park to enjoy our meal. It felt heavenly to sit in the sunshine, listening to the birdsong and smelling the fresh grass. It would be a long time before I took the sounds and odours for granted. I nearly cried at how much those insignificant things mattered, how much I had missed them. Being cut off from the world I knew and out of touch with all that was familiar had affected me deeper than I thought possible.

The bench faced a pond where we watched the swans drift along and the locals fed the geese. All seemed normal, like we belonged right here, right now, and for the moment I just was. I savoured every sensation from the gentlest breeze to the warm, gooey cheese. It was a marvellous moment. But we couldn't stay for long.

"So where to now, my lady?" Jack forced the words out around a mouthful of pepperoni. With grease dripping down his chin, the rivulets in the dirt were becoming less attractive.

"Any hotel that will take a pair like us" I quipped as I wiped the mess off from his face with a napkin from the bag. It did not help. It made a smear that looked like old coffee grounds. Realizing we would be lucky to not be arrested, let alone find a room for the night, we set off to find a place to rest.

Choices

"Good afternoon, princess." It was not the smell of fragrant flowers, but the heady aroma of hamburgers and fries that came through the door ahead of Jack and his voice. A very unladylike growl from my stomach answered for me as I struggled to sit up, my groans adding to the protest. "It's a beautiful day in the neighbourhood!"

Another groan left my lips as the song started looping in my brain. My eyes opened long enough to focus on the proffered bag of food. Reaching for my meal, I got my first look at the damage our last adventure had wrought on my arm. Tipping my hand to get a better view of the swelling and the bruises, Jack did the same, rotating my wrist, marvelling at the interesting patterns that were visible with the dust washed away.

"That's gonna hurt," Jack stated the obvious. I hadn't been aware of the pain until he pointed it out. I would have slugged him if there wasn't a chance something else might get damaged. Seeing my glare, Jack stepped out of reach, his hip movement showing he had not escaped unscathed himself.

"We might be too old for this shit," I said in reply, the sarcasm dripping as thickly as Jack's pizza grease had done the night before. I opened the bag and took out my lunch, setting out the food as though I needed to do inventory first.

Jack snorted, nearly spilling his meal. We both settled in to eat, the day quickly vanishing, and we had yet to make any progress on our quest. Sitting back with a sigh of contentment, I watched Jack's movements. Everything he does, he does to perfection. Even with the shadows darkening his eyes, the hollows emphasizing the stress we have been under, Jack was still the most handsome man I had ever been with. Ever. Catching the look in my eye, Jack finished his meal, then stood before me and took my hand.

Pulling me to my feet, Jack slowly embraced me, understanding that this was not the time to rush. That our bodies needed to come together gently, with care and finesse. While we are usually prone to the bull-in-a-china-shop method of intercourse, our battered state called for us to linger as each stage fired our passion until the pain was no longer an obstacle. The slow burn ignited, and we lost ourselves in the flames for a soul-filling moment, tangled together and in the sheets. And we slept.

I woke up for the second time, still wrapped in the covers, once more alone. I stretched, relishing the tightness and the tenderness, evidence of our lovemaking. Sleeping deeply, I had not even noticed when he left the bed, not heard him leave the room. Swinging my legs over the side of the bed, I dragged the sheet with me as I went to the window to look out into the night sky. Flashes of neon broadcast the latest Broadway blockbuster and a dozen billboards lit up the street. People walked and hurried like ants, all moving in ever-blending rivers of humanity, scurrying from one stoplight to the next.

Realizing Jack had most likely gone out to bring us more food, I spent a pleasant minute wondering what delight he would think of. In a city like New York, the choices are endless. But our funds weren't. If I wanted to get paid for my services, we would have to work out this puzzle. Sighing, I turned from the lighted spectacle and prepared to go over what we learned during our visit to Elarenah's realm. This might be a serious challenge as I thought Jack was recording everything, so I hadn't paid a lot of attention, other than learning how to trigger the portal. Steeling myself against the discomfort, I pulled the Book from its hiding place, breathing through the pinch as it released its hold and became tangible once more.

Jack entered just as the Book solidified. Setting our treasure aside to dig into the feast he had brought, I set about explaining what I had seen before the werewolf tried to dismember me, all the while gesturing with my chopsticks. Rice flew about the room and I giggled. The tension of the past few days melted away, and we changed topics to talk about anything and everything except our mission, pretending to be normal people having a normal meal. Our lives don't need to be go-go-go all the time. Our dinner wrapped up with a quick kiss before I dug my bag out from under the bed.

My notebook held the sequence we needed to reopen the Book and to see the hologram I witnessed before everything went sideways. Our trash set aside, Jack pulled out some paper and scribbled down the bits of information as I recalled them. Not trying to make sense of them yet. I knew he would sort them all out later, finding the edges and building a complete picture without an image to go by. Therein lies his magick. Once he has a clue trail to follow, he is unstoppable. And now that we are in our world, Jack is in his glory. His contacts, his resources, his research are all back.

"And you glimpsed a portal before everything fell apart?" Jack questioned as he tried to make sense of the rambling path my memories had taken.

"That's what it seemed to be. There was a glimmer. Like you could almost touch it, but not. At the same time." Jack is accustomed to me not speaking clearly, but the confusion on his face told me this was harder than most times. "The surface looked like a bubble, an almost clear texture. Like it would pop if you looked at it too closely. In fact, it was easier to see if you looked at it sideways. Maybe focusing on it is a trigger to increase the security, make it more difficult to see." Now Jack was thoroughly confused since he hadn't been in the room the first time.

Deciding the only way to make this entire experience make sense was to bring the image back to life, I folded myself into a seated position on the floor with the Book laid on my lap. The carvings were more detailed this time, depicting scenes never seen before. As I turned it over in my hands, the story revealed itself. Vaguely familiar images appeared, and I dropped it as if my fingers had been burned. Astonishment and fear flickered through my mind as the Book fell partway to the floor to float lazily below my outstretched hands.

Jack crouched to inspect it.

"Well, that's new." He reached out to stroke the cover, only to have the Book slide away. Amused to find himself playing tag with an inanimate object, Jack tried again, but a ward shielded it from him. Maybe it remembered the episode with the shape-shifter and was protecting itself. This Book was so much more than we ever imagined. I frowned as I wondered if it may also take the step of initiating a defence, and I reached out to bring Jack's hand away from it.

Working on the theory that the Book possessed magick of its own, I bent down to peer under and around it, looking for telltale signs it was internally generating the wards. As before, I only saw the magick out of the corner of my eye, like fairy wings in their gossamer appearance. Fragile strands of magick shimmered just within the reach of human sight, appearing and disappearing as the energy flowed. Experimenting, I used my finger to enter the protective sphere around the book, this time paying attention to the forces I encountered. I closed my eyes, limiting the impulses my mind had to filter through and concentrated instead on the messages I was receiving.

Jack watched my face as I worked through the delicate procedure of unravelling the security system we had activated, or more accurately, the werewolf had activated. The Book did not understand Jack was not the enemy it encountered before, and I needed to make that happen. As a test, I sent out a directive, filling its field with loving intention, an effective technique when used in the right place and at the right time. As I communicated with it, the energy began shifting and adjusting, like thought waves taking an alternate route. This was unfamiliar territory. Despite carrying the Book for so long, I had never once thought to join myself with it as it had with me. Until now, it had been nothing more than a package to be protected. I had not perceived the Book as a living record of the Universe, changing and evolving as events unfolded. Until now, I had not understood how important this tome was, how dangerous in the wrong hands.

As the Book accepted my energy and felt the truth behind my intentions, I began receiving glimpses of knowledge, memories resurfacing, pulling forward thoughts and feelings lost long ago. After a century of living, there is much to forget, much you don't want to remember, and much you wish you could do again. All this, and more, cycled through my mind as I allowed the Book to absorb everything about me, about Jack, and about our mission. In the blink of my mind's eye, all I had ever done in this life and more were reviewed, judged, and returned to their former place. The pain, the sorrow, the grief — all there and gone again in a flash. All the love, the joy, the achievements — all flashed before me like the windows of a speeding train, too fast to see as individual images or memories, leaving only their impressions behind.

With the assessment complete, I sensed the wards shrinking, dissipating back into the pool of magick held deep within the Book. Confident it would no longer reject him, I opened my eyes and nodded at Jack to try again. As he did so, I turned my hands beneath the volume to catch it should the Book fall. With my understanding came a bigger reverence for what I was holding onto. With all we had been through, it was a good thing I didn't know then what I know now. Remembering some of our more dangerous times, like this morning, I'm not sure I would have been so cavalier had I been more aware of the value or the risk.

Jack's hand grazed the leather, and I felt the Book shudder for a moment, then relax as it realized Jack meant no harm. It seemed surreal to be thinking of it as a living thing, not just magick enchanted, but it had all the characteristics, short of breathing, and it was definitely cognizant. As Jack drifted his hand down the spine, we could hear a deep rumble, like the murmur of an impending storm. I almost expected the cover to arch up like the back of a cat, begging to be scratched a little more. Satisfied it had removed the wards, I grasped the sides of the Book and tenderly brought it back to my lap.

Eyes wide, Jack pulled his hands back and wonder crossed his face as he too realized the importance, the splendour, the genuine power in the pages. The story was still being written, still changing, the knowledge being added to as we sat in our room. That so much could exist in something so small was jaw-dropping. With that knowledge came more than a little fear, as we now had a better understanding of what our leaders were after. This book was not some relic to be donated to a museum and put on display. This was not a simple archaeological treasure for the masses to read and stare at in a glass case.

The fact of the matter was that we had been lied to. Manipulated, pulled, chased and damn near killed so either the Council or the Assembly would come out the winner. This was never about collecting history. This was about controlling the Universe and everything in it. With this book and advanced knowledge of magick, a practitioner could perceivably travel to any place and time and alter the outcome to benefit their party. This was about being the supreme ruler of all that was in the known, and some of the unknown galaxies, planets, and star systems. Their inhabitants were simple sentient beings, going about their lives, not aware of the galactic fight for domination raging in the Universe.

I sat stewing about the implications before sharing my ideas with Jack. I had never considered keeping it before now. We had a job to do — get the Book, protect it from the Ferin, figure out how to read it, then return it to the Assembly. As a Universal Guard, they gave me my orders. I mean, the bonus for completing the mission was a big one, one I eagerly expected. Who wouldn't? Okay, I may have glanced over the fine print. Nobody reads every word. It's why they make the contracts so damn long and full of words no one understands. Maybe the legalese would trip me up this time. But knowing what I know now, I can't take this Book of Knowledge back to the Assembly. And I can't allow the Council to get their hands on it. Stalemate. Stuck in the middle again...

Lesser of Two Evils

"You know that there is no good ending to this, right Steph?" Jack ran his fingers through his tousled hair for about the fortieth time in the past hour. His pacing marked his passage from wall to wall as he looked at our dilemma from every angle and view.

I sighed, confident if there had been an easy way out, Jack would have spotted it by now.

"Figured as much. Why can't there ever be a simple way to obstruct Universal domination? Why does there always need to be some galactic blow-up, monumental fallout, and mass destruction?" Most of those questions were rhetorical, but I felt like we were in the middle of a movie with no good guys to run home to, no quartermaster in our corner giving us gadgets…

Hold that thought.

The look on my face was enough to stop Jack from making another rut on the carpet and stood waiting for me to finish taking my thought train to the station.

We've wondered how the Ferin track us all the time. We know the Guard keeps a lock on us through Jack's TC, but there are curious gaps in coverage where his computer works and when the Ferin can still locate us. For instance, we have been on our Earth for a day now and found no sign of intruders. No unexplained light shows, no mass panic and death on the streets, no ripple in the energy. Maybe there is a technological 'dead zone', pre-programmed gaps to give us places and times of rest, room to make sense of the mystery. In the past, we have had days of quiet when we could sort out parts of the puzzle, found access to libraries and archives to gain the knowledge we needed to move the pieces around on the board. It was only as we got close to understanding anything that they found us again.

So who has a bigger stake in this?

Who wants the knowledge known yet not used?

Who wants us to understand the exceptional power and keep it contained?

What if we have an ally?

There is more to be revealed, but I am catching glimmers of what is going on. Elarenah had hinted at the Book when we talked. She must have sensed it when we arrived. Her reticence at my announcement about being a part of the Universal Guard, her sudden need to see within my mind, her deceptive manoeuvre with the shape-shifter—what if these were an attempt to retrieve the Book?

What if the Book of Knowledge was Fae created?

What if the Fae were not our enemy, but rather that they saw us as their enemy? Did that make sense??

What if Elarenah felt compelled to take the Book to protect it from the Assembly <u>and</u> the Council? Now that we have figured out who the players are and what the prize is, what if we are actually on the same side?

My shoulders slumped as I reached the only logical conclusion. Jack will not be pleased when I suggest we seek out Elarenah and her remaining henchmen.

Playing with the Enemy

everal hours and many drinks later, Jack and I had hashed out all the options, thoughts, misgivings, and concerns about our predicament and came back to needing a powerhouse in our corner. There was no other obvious choice. We could not hold the line against the Council and the Assembly at the same time. We can barely do it when we only have a handful of Ferin agents after us. Okay, sometimes it has been a whole military unit, but when stacked up against the bulk of their forces? We might as well dig our own graves and be done with it.

And the Assembly. I've trained with them, shared meals and quarters, and understand the fervour they will be in when I break ranks. There is no going back once I declare myself to be against the Assembly. When I denounce the Guard, I place a target on my back. It will bring out the wrath of all those I have bested, along with all those who felt I never belonged. Their satisfaction at being right will outweigh their reasoning and push aside any thought of questioning why I would leave after I had fought so hard to get in.

And understanding the structure, the upper echelon would

seed rumours of my treachery with lies and supposition, making me out to be a blackguard, quickly ruining my good name to protect their own. My life, my reputation, was about to go up in flames. There was no way around it. All I had built was nothing compared to all that was to be lost if either group gained control of this book. My reputation meant nothing when compared to the lives of every living thing in the Universe. I have never felt so insignificant, not even floating alone in the Atlantic Ocean in the dark. The vastness of what was being affected by this decision weighed so heavily that I slipped into a moment of abject misery, grieving for the loss of all that had come before, all that we had fought for, all that we had known or thought we knew to be true. With tears streaming down my face, Jack hugged me until the sobs subsided and I found the words to explain how the train got from point A to point Z.

Jack let me finish my pity party before wiping my cheeks with his fingers. Gently holding my face in his hands, he kissed away the remaining salt from my lips. Never one to overlook an opportunity, Jack edged his hands down my body as the kiss deepened and the heat grew. As his fingertips brushed the sides of my breasts, the tiniest gasp escaped between our joined mouths, enough to let him know I would welcome more of his attention, if only for a distraction from the earth-shattering escapade facing us beyond the closed doors of our hotel room.

For the moment, it could be just the two of us. As if nothing else mattered. For the moment, I couldn't think of anything better. Together, we rocked our world for the better part of the evening, moving our embrace from the floor to the bed and, later, to the shower. The steam and flowing water added to the sensory overload that kept all other thoughts at bay for the rest of the night, allowing us to slip into a dreamless state, tangled up in the sheets we tossed aside in our fevered motions. Needing only each other for warmth, we slept until dawn, safe, if only for those few hours.

A timid knock on the door announced the arrival of our breakfast. Jack had wisely arranged for a meal, knowing my stomach would roar for attention when I woke up. I am not a sleeping beauty by any means. If there is a picture of a wind-tossed squirrel somewhere, I closely resemble that squirrel when I roll out of bed. With my hair splayed out like I had survived a hurricane, Jack chuckled at me as he always does and shooed me off to the mirror to scare myself.

You would think I could learn a spell to tame my mane, but all I have ever been able to do was make it grow. And right now, my hair looked like I was growing space to house birds in. Basic stuff, Stephanie. Do the basic stuff. How hard is it to brush your hair? I rummaged through my pack to find my hairbrush. My fingers skimmed over the other contents and came across something unfamiliar. Coming back out into the bedroom, I dumped my bag out on the bed, hoping not to lose anything in the jumbled sheets. Jack lifted an eyebrow as I had not yet made any attempt at toning down the brambles. I sorted through the pile of bits and baubles, pulling aside the items I knew to be mine until one remained. Stepping back from the bed, I raised my finger to my lips and glanced back to the bathroom.

"Honey, you really should do something with your hair. It looks like you walked five miles through a sandstorm." Jack said, playing up the whole messy look.

"Just need to grab my brush and I'll try to do something with it," I replied with a dash of sarcasm. I picked up my things from the bed, throwing most of them back in the bag, including my little stowaway. Then I flounced off.

Jack followed me in stealth mode and turned on the water. He arched his eyebrow again. One of these days I'm going to figure out how to do that and look cool at the same time. Not wanting to risk being overheard, I resorted to mind-speak while I continued to work the tangles out of my hair.

'I don't know what that thing is or when it was placed in my bag, but it would certainly explain how the Ferin were able to find us earlier.'

'If it is a tracking device. I'll need to inspect it. That could be tricky if it has the capability of eavesdropping as well.'

'How do you want to handle things? We can hardly go around not speaking anymore just because we found a bug in my bag.'

'No, that's not practical, but maybe we can use this to our advantage. Knowing your enemy is listening helps you to plan evasively. If we can hamper the tracking portion and leave the rest active, we should be able to give them something to do for a while.' Jack's face split into a wide grin as the wheels started spinning, a scheme already taking shape. *'First, one of us needs to take a*

shower though, just to keep up appearances.' Somehow that meant a soaking was in my future as the next thing I knew, Jack scooped me up and dropped me in the tub. Spluttering under the water, I may have screamed a little girly scream, which, of course, gave Jack the reason he needed to pretend to come in and save me.

I hope whoever was listening to us enjoyed the show. Jack made a big production out of it. I can't say I didn't enjoy the episode myself. For the record, there was soap and an overflow of bubbles involved. And I may have screamed a little more. Okay. A lot more. Enough that the neighbours next to us banged on the wall and yelled at us to keep it down. This sent me off in a fit of giggles, relieving any remaining tension and making me as soft and fluid as a warm cup of cocoa.

Knowing we were being monitored made me determined to embarrass our eavesdroppers. Maybe they had heard it all before. Maybe we could teach them something new. And maybe they weren't listening at all. Whatever the case, if they were keeping tabs on us, they were about to listen to an afternoon full of snoring and not much of consequence. I curled up in bed, settling in with little more than my thoughts and some cold toast. Jack wanted to take some time to go over his notes and monitor the bug himself, try to tap in remotely with his TC. I have never thoroughly understood what that thing was, but it has more functions than any smartphone I have ever seen.

Jack moved off to the bathroom to reduce any noise he might

make tapping away on his screen. Exhaustion soon overtook me, and I drifted off to a fitful sleep, memories and visions warring with thoughts and dreams until I jolted awake. The room was dark, and Jack was asleep beside me. That I had not felt him climb into bed told me how tired I had been. I was grateful he had left me sleeping, even if it meant missing a meal or two. At the moment, however, sleep would not come back, the images playing over and over in my mind's eye making it impossible.

Hidden in the jumble of riddles and pictograms, symbols and phrases was the answer we were seeking. My brain had spent its last few hours rearranging the clues and flashing them in an internal movie, trying things this way and that until there was sense to be made. It did not feel complete yet, but I was closing in on something. Now to hold on to it for longer than half a second. Knowing that grabbing at smoke made it harder to catch, I eased my way out of bed and rummaged around for any leftovers.

I really had been out of it. Tucked in the fridge were an apple and a deli meat sandwich. Jack must have gone for a walk before crashing beside me. Taking my spoils and a bottle of water, I attempted to settle into the lotus position on the floor. It felt like months since I last meditated, and the physical trauma I had suffered made attaining the right balance slightly difficult and moderately painful. Muscles and joints refused to stretch and move in need of a warm-up first. I was trying to let Jack sleep, so my normal routine was out of the question. Yoga worked to loosen up the knots in my back and legs. I smiled, remembering how some of those knots got there. The tightness slipped from between my shoulders. As I rolled the vertebrae in my neck and spine, a loud 'pop' and the resulting shift in my muscles had me groaning again, this time in comfort as the pain and stress melted away.

My knees folded more gently this time and without protest. Finally comfortable, I munched on my midnight snack, satisfying the dragon that lives in my belly. The familiar position helped me to relax further, my hands upright on my legs. The trick to meditation is monitoring your breath, allowing your mind to enter the in-between state where yogi and spiritual practitioners go when they relinquish their ties to their mortal bodies. Inhaling deeper now, I slowly let go, the rhythm of my breath becoming the backdrop to my heartbeat. Both quietly did their jobs while I stepped out into the nothingness that lies beyond our reality.

Into the Void

There is a strangeness about turning back and seeing yourself sitting motionless, but for your chest rising and falling. How your body can keep rigidity and sit with no conscious effort from your brain. In stepping out, I have taken control of my essence and we are about to embark on a walk through the Universe. I took a moment to hover over Jack as he lay sprawled across the covers. My instincts were to reach out and cover him up, tuck him in for his well-deserved rest. Without my body, the best I could do was brush a kiss across his cheek, the energy able to leave a signature. Jack moved his hand up to touch my mark, then snuggled in deeper, a gentle smile curving his lips.

Feeling certain he would sleep for a few hours, I returned to my task. The pieces of the puzzle would be easier to see here. I could hold and manipulate them into place, discard them if unnecessary. All things have meaning, just not for the here-and-now. Tricky beings, these ancients. Nothing is ever done in a straight line. We never know if something we learn is important or not. Ultimately, all the knowledge will be used. It's the when that is hard to decipher.

The challenge for the moment is that only my data is available to work with. Jack stores much of the information on his TC, often background bits that only come to light when I ask specific questions. For now, I would have to build my puzzle without all the pieces, hoping for enough edges to start. At least I now possessed a picture to recreate. Our visit with Elarenah gave me a glimpse into the life of the Fae and all the other ancients as it was in the time before time. Deep in my mind were memories of cities, people, buildings, and libraries. The images were being recreated on the Book of Knowledge, raising the imprint in the leather, though they had yet to appear on the pages. Looking back, they had always been present. I was previously without the ability to see them clearly. It's like one of the Magic Eye puzzles where everything is out of focus until you figure out the image. And once you have seen it, you can't unsee it. Now that I knew the history of Otherworld for myself, the reliefs in the leather came smoothly into view.

Holding fast to what I had seen, I pulled together all I remembered from our previous missions, the last few weeks, the orders we had received, and the knowledge which was now inherent in me from my chat with Elarenah. As I stood in the middle of my circle of imagery, I turned counter-clockwise first, letting my mind sort through everything and sort it by relative importance.

The images were sometimes pleasant as they showed me the way of life for all inhabitants before the Uprising. As more and more pictures flooded my brain, I noticed subtle shifts in the imagery, telltale signs of external manipulation. As I would reach for a particular piece, it might be easy to grab or it might wink out of existence again. I felt as though I was playing chess against a master who stayed three steps ahead, trying to outmanoeuvre me. Stepping away from my intended mission, the recreation of the cover and the translation of the Book, I took the time to meet the challenge as presented. Time to remove the mask and play for keeps.

Even as pure energy, I usually keep the form I present in my everyday life — Stephanie, the willowy brunette, slowly moving from young and innocent to mature and vital. Over time, it has become apparent that I am so much more than just a human. I seldom let my true energetic being show, as the impact is hard on my companions. I had shown Elarenah, for she needed to understand I was not to be trifled with, though she tried anyway. Jack has seen glimpses of it on a couple of occasions when I wanted to gain a psychological edge. I keep it well hidden, for great fear has shown in Jack's eyes when I reveal my truest form and I will not scare him off. My life would have no meaning without him.

But here? Here I am alone with the Universe and its maker. Here I can be myself without judgment or reservation. With that decision, I released the last vestige of my persona, of 'Stephanie' and opened up my energy to embody what I have rejected for so long.

As humans, we think of the continent of Atlantis as being the centre of all knowledge in the ancient world. And mostly, we are right. What I am starting to understand is the island we have named Atlantis was merely an Earthbound portal from the Otherworld, much like the one between Elarenah's world and our Earth. The access to Otherworld slammed shut when the Uprising caused the worlds to separate, the people and other beings to be scattered, the knowledge lost to all but a few. The chaos of war demolished the city and its inhabitants, leaving little behind but rubble and genetic memories.

And me.

That long, cold, dark night when I nearly froze to death in the Atlantic was my trigger. In my moment of crisis, my DNA flipped a switch, activating long dormant strands which changed me from the human I was born as, into the being I had always been. And here, in the openness of space and time, in the in-between, I have finally and fully acknowledged this integral part of myself, the ancient being long sheltered behind my physical facade.

Time moves differently in the in-between, and not knowing how long remained before Jack woke up, I rushed to confirm my suspicions. If I took it slow, my inner chicken would get in the way. It was one thing to suspect what I was. And what I was capable of. But doubt had always made me second-guess my feelings, my memories. I was human, after all — wasn't I? I had accepted the differences in my face when I showed my other side. But where to look now? Trusting my intuition to guide me and starting with the most obvious thought, I reached around to drag my fingers along the space between my shoulder blades and down my back. While I had sensed nothing out of place in my human body, there had always been a density, like extra muscle. This next decision would change everything I knew about myself. Taking a figurative deep breath, I pushed against the heaviness, unleashing the energy that had been packed away.

Confirming what I now embodied yet not understood, or wanted to believe, I gave in to the need clawing at my very soul. My wings, tucked so long against my spine as to have been invisible in real life, unfurled with all the subtly of an orchestral symphony. Freedom came with the release, as though my energy could flow more freely. My extremities extended, and the channels reopened. I arched my shoulders back, allowing the weight to pull them down towards my feet, stretching the new muscles. It took time for my aura to move around my wings, caress them, bathe them in healing and strengthen them until they hung perfectly balanced, as though they had always been.

While in our meeting, Elarenah had determined what I truly was, yet never gave it away. Until now, I had not, nor would I have, believed it. I had seen glimmers of the truth in the past, minor things that when taken individually meant nothing, but meant so much more when viewed together on the chessboard. Just as some people are good and others are evil, so are there beings of greater power that choose one path or another. Titles established by people to differentiate them often miss the nuances in personalities and lump like-featured beings into one category over another. Characteristics are assigned and rarely altered as people decide how others should behave.

Standing tall, I revelled in watching my wings shift and move as they pleased. The deepest purple blended with the emeralds, indigoes, and blacks as deep as galactic space itself. Each feather was a display of artwork, no two shimmering the same way in the light of a thousand stars. My path had followed my personality as well as my genetically induced preferences. While I developed a strong moral and ethical set of rules, I would not hesitate to destroy obstacles to my purpose. I was definitely not all 'love and light'. I am most comfortable in the darkness, walking in the shadows where I blend in, where my true colours could shine, even when they could not be seen.

Without my knowledge, my wings had protected me more than once, shading me from heat, hiding me in darker shadows. Answer after answer for inexplicable actions came clicking into place as I recalled instances where death came calling, yet I lived to tell the tale. My hand reached for the scar just above my left kidney, a souvenir from a knife plunged deep into my body, a thrust designed to end my life. I recall questioning the Universe about my survival. At the time, I was not to know the role I would be playing. Nor of the level of protection laying dormant within my body.

Had I known about my true self at any point, had I known I was even less mortal, I would have been more reckless than I already was. The knowledge of what I am had been kept from me for very good reasons. Now that I have the maturity to use the knowledge wisely, it looked like I had passed the right test, for the pieces came fast and furious, filling in the blanks as they went with only a few open holes remaining. Perhaps these were Jack's to know. Our lives were interwoven on many levels, the most valuable being the current dilemma.

As the pictures formed around me, my brain diligently absorbed all it could. I simultaneously adjusted my thoughts about who, and what, I am. Next would be the difficult task of sharing it all with Jack. The true test of trust. Did I trust him with all the knowledge about me? He has sworn to kill all beasts and creatures known to harm humans. There is a fury that overtakes him when all reason has left, and he sees nothing but death and destruction.

While I have found comfort in accepting the last piece of myself, I mourned the loss of what we had. A shiver of fear coursed through me with the premonition that all I needed, all I had lived for, was about to crash around me. Weeping in the emptiness of space, my tears sparkled like diamonds in the starlight. I cried for all that had been. I cried for all that might yet be. And I cried for those who would never know love as I have.

And as I wept, I knew. I knew Jack had chosen me as I was, even the parts he could not see with his physical eyes. For a moment, I had forgotten he, too, was more than human. That I had chosen to love and be loved by a man who had also been changed into something no other human would accept. I allowed the last tears to fall away. The fear fell with them and the last doubt that lay between us fell, too. I was whole.

Faith

Morning broke much too soon for my liking. I would have been perfectly content to stay cuddled up in bed with Jack and never show my face in public again. Not exactly practical, but a happy little dream that made me smile just for a moment. Then the enormity of the secret I had to share today crashed into me, causing me to start and wake Jack. He stretched like a leopard preparing to climb down from his lofty perch. Watching the muscles ripple beneath his marked skin, I tried, unsuccessfully, to keep the grief from pushing me to cry yet again.

Jack opened his eyes to see my tear-swollen face, bringing him instantly to a mild panic, thinking he had slept through something catastrophic. Concern flashed across his face as he sprung to his feet and grabbed my shoulders, checking for damage. Finding no apparent cause for the tears, he sat back on the bed and arched that famous eyebrow in question. Choking on my emotions, I crouched on the floor and bowed my head as grief and fear warred for supremacy over my heart.

Upon returning to my body in the wee hours of the night, I had pulled my wings and newly expanded energy back into their familiar shape and form. The one Jack was accustomed to seeing. I had slept erratically, pretending to be the human being Jack fell asleep beside last night. Now the truth, that I was no longer the same person, strained at my soul. As much as we changed over the decades, we did it together, growing as a couple, altering and adjusting as life put challenges before us. This was out of that realm. This was so life-altering as to be a deal-breaker. No simple way came to mind that would help me tell the tale. Dragging in a breath, I brought as much focus to the here-and-now as I could muster. Exhaling the nerves, watching my hands shake in my lap, I decided there was no simple path to take, no soft serve method to make this any easier.

Slowly, with dread bearing down on me, I straightened up before turning my back to Jack. This was one of those times when I wished I didn't sleep naked, desperate for a blanket or a towel to wrap up in. But it would only delay the inevitable. One more deep sigh and I straightened to my full height. Setting my mind to it, I rolled my shoulders forward and back, feeling my way to the most comfortable stance. Fingers of fear crawled along my spine. I pushed through it, praying it would all turn out right. Despite my faith in Jack, I prepared for the possibility of battle, for the attack that may head my way once I revealed my true form.

Shielding my heart and knowing there was no more to wait for, I dropped the last of my resistance. My wings unfurled from my back, gracefully fluffing out to their full width before settling into a comfortable position. I watched as several tiny feathers drifted to the carpet and stood motionless, focusing on the woven pattern while Jack processed what had just happened.

"Can you put those away now? I can't see your ass with them hanging there like that."

I whirled around, flabbergasted that Jack had nothing more to say about two gigantic appendages appearing in front of him. Stunned would be an excellent word. After all my angst about how he would react, Jack's only response was to stare at my ass.

More feathers floated about the room, caught up in the whirlwind created when I spun about. Too afraid to ask, I tried arching an eyebrow. Still can't do it. My alternative was to put one hand on my hip and use the other to gesture for Jack to continue, to say something — anything — to ask the questions racing through his mind.

All I did, apparently, was to turn up the heat. Standing there with one hip cocked, wings bracketing my bare body, and my hand extended in his direction was all the invitation Jack needed to stand up in his full glory. With a steamy look in his eyes, Jack stepped into my space, bending down to kiss me with a passion I hadn't known I was craving. The fire coursed through my body, a groan of pleasure from my throat giving Jack more encouragement. We let our bodies do the talking as we explored and touched and moved each other in ways we had perfected over the years.

Until I forgot about my wings and, in a moment of excitement, turned too quickly. The next moment found us tangled up on the floor, feathers flying everywhere and Jack groaning. One hand was holding his head where I had clocked him. I rolled onto my stomach, letting my wings cover us both as I laughed uncontrollably, more tears staining the carpet. Jack curled up next to me under the make-shift blanket and kissed my cheek. The moment had passed. We would have another one. And that was all I needed to know right now.

Tucking my wings in, still more comfortable with them hidden, I hurried off to take a shower and get dressed for a day of research. They had never accosted us on Earth in our timeline, but with the end of the quest drawing close, all bets could be off. The Assembly would want an update, and not knowing when the Council would send the Ferin around to roust us, it was time to focus on getting answers out of the Book. More and more doubts crept in about giving this relic to anyone. There was so much more to be unlocked, and we needed to see what mysteries remained concealed.

Under the door came the aroma of fried bacon and buttered toast. YEAH! In my absence, Jack had ordered breakfast. And lunch. Does he know me, or what? Devouring my food while Jack took his turn in the shower, I looked around and noticed a pile of feathers placed on the end of the bed. The colours danced and played as I watched, the shimmer still vibrant though it was beginning the fade. I took a larger feather and went to stand by the window; the light bringing out variations and revealing patterns buried within the black. Staring at one particular symbol, I felt myself being drawn into it and began tracing the lines with my finger. The image glowed and rose like a holograph. Twisting it this way and that, I tried to make sense of what it was showing me, with no more luck than I had with the Book. Deciding to just accept the beauty of it, I filed it away as another puzzle for another day. If I ever have a quiet moment to work on all my puzzles, I think I will need a year just to catalogue them all, let alone sort out any of the pieces.

Finishing my tea, I sat down with our notes and tried to make sense of Jack's hen-scratching. Even turning them the wrong way up didn't help. It would have to wait. And the waiting made me antsy. I began pacing, marking more grooves in the carpet as I went. But the movement helped get the thoughts flowing. I let my mind replay the image from the Faerie princess's hotel room, rotating it every which way until I had a light-bulb moment. I closed my eyes to focus more intently on the memory. Each small section shone briefly before fading back into the shadows. The images sped up, and I struggled to keep up with the flow of information. My breath quickened as I mentally raced to retain as much as possible, not taking even a second to scribble anything down. I prayed I could relate everything to Jack later.

As quickly as they started, the images stopped. And no matter what I did, they would not move again. I had reached the point I had access to and could go no further. At least I had another clue to what we were searching for.

Confident I was on the right track, but not trusting myself to write everything down accurately, I scrambled to find Jack's recording device. In a jumble, the words poured out of my mouth and into the ether. Jack entered the room as I was speaking, drawn by the unusual sound of my voice. His jaw dropped open. The opulence and beauty I depicted invoked a scene that filled him with awe and joy. And then confusion crossed his face as my voice and tone changed. I stared at Jack's face in puzzlement. He sat back, uncertainty in his eyes.

"And what language was that?"

I blinked. "English??"

"Some of it. The ending? Not so much." Jack crossed the room and came to sit beside me on the bed. "You were describing a library when I came in. Then, in the middle of a sentence, your voice and cadence changed. You didn't even stop. It was like you didn't even hear your own words."

My turn to be puzzled. In my mind, I spoke in English. Why would I speak a different language? If it were French or Spanish, he would have said so. For me to use words neither of us knew was more than strange. To talk as though it was my native tongue moved us into an additional dimension of 'odd'. For me to do so and not know it happened? That added a new level of bizarre. First, wings. Now, an unfamiliar language. I shook my head to see if it would make more sense, but it did nothing more than rattle my brain around.

Shrugging my shoulder as the only answer I had, I picked up the recorder. Maybe listening to my words would help me understand. In the meantime, Jack grabbed his notebook and madly scratched what he remembered from my recitation.

Hoping he recalled enough and could eventually decipher his scribbling, I backed up the recording to push play.

Knock, knock, knock.

"Housekeeping."

Turning off the recorder and stuffing everything into the bag, I scurried about grabbing feathers and anything else that looked out of place as Jack moved to the door. He looked at me as he put his hand on his pistol and signalled for me to back away and be quiet. Thinking back, the "Do Not Disturb" sign should be hanging on the doorknob, and we had not checked out, so who was knocking on our door? It sure wasn't the maid.

Trepidation fell heavily in the pit of my stomach. In my rush to record the details, I had forgotten about the bug. Shaking my head at my ineptitude, I scrambled into my jacket, grabbing up Jack's as I went. The corner was my only refuge. I took one last look around the room, seeing nothing left behind but the tangle of bed sheets. If it was the maid, it was their problem. What were the odds that it was really housekeeping?

Knock, knock, knock. This time, the knob turned, rattling as the person on the other side tested the lock.

Jack took up his position beside the door, fully prepared to do some damage to whoever opened it.

"Now, Stephanie. Don't make me come through this door." The voice carried a ring of familiarity, but in my heightened state, I was hard-pressed to know from where.

"You didn't think you could keep hiding from me, from us, did you? Although your little stunt at the hospital was impressive."

The Ferin scout! Damn it. Time's up.

The scout was obviously pacing in the hallway; the shadow moving back and forth under the door. Her steps grew more agitated as we stayed locked up in our room, temporarily safe behind the walls and our warding. We were at a stalemate. Jack retreated to cover me as best he could in the compact space.

'Suggestions?'

'Nothing short of a nuclear bomb is going to get them out of that hallway.' I sent back, miffed at having been located already. *'We need an exit strategy.'*

"You know I can sense your fear, right?" she purred against the door. "Your scent is so tasty, like strawberry jam on ice cream." Her voice oozed through the door like an oil spill tainting our room, inviting itself into our minds. I could almost taste the words. The magick they contained was palpable. This was no ordinary scout, but a well-trained magickian, couching her spell as she crafted it. She hoped her implications would distract us and I would miss the real incantation encrypted as she spoke.

'I need to double our wards. She is spell-casting and I need to make

it backfire.'

Jack nodded his agreement and stepped to the side to give me room to do my thing. Drawing my magick into the game, I sensed the scout zero in on my position, a necessary risk. Good magick should never be rushed, but we were out of options. Nuclear it is.

Piggybacking on her incantation, I drew in as much of the scout's magick as I could handle. Its greasy texture made me cringe as I absorbed the vileness and contained it in the spell I was weaving. When I felt a shift in the balance, when I felt her withdrawal, when I felt the game change, I propelled a wave of magick back to the starting point. Following the trail back to its maker, dragging the darkness with it, my counter-spell slammed into the scout, coupled with an intention I had hoped to never use again.

I have spent a lot of time coming to terms with the fact that I kill other living beings. I would say 'people', but they haven't always been human. And while the Ferin can be human-like, they have changed to be something more. I have killed in defence of my own life. I have killed in defence of those I love. Today, I might take out some innocent humans currently sleeping in the rooms surrounding us, blissfully unaware that their time on Earth is short.

The end of the Ferin was almost inconsequential. With the door in between, we did not receive the full effect of the blast or its blowback. Jack shielded me from the debris that flew into the room when the door disintegrated, but by then, little remained of anything previously standing outside of our room. There was barely anything left of the hallway. Emergency lighting flickered and sirens wailed. We brushed off the particles of wood and plaster and picked our way through the remnants of our room. Stepping through the falling doorway, we plastered dazed looks on our faces before melding into the crowds of hotel patrons rushing to escape. In the confusion, we made our way to the street and faded into the chaos collecting on the sidewalk outside.

Destination Unknown

Avoiding the incoming professionals, we moved off to a small park to watch the ensuing reorganization as police and paramedics arrived, taking control of the situation in their usual well-planned way. More sirens announced the firetrucks, and the firefighters took their turn at clearing the rest of the building. There was nothing more to do here. Jack took my hand, and we sent a silent prayer to any victims of our magickians' battle. We had no evidence the scout was out of the game, or the Ferin who waited with her in the hallway. I did know they found here us, on our home planet, in our own time, and the anger built within me. Jack squeezed my hand, sensing the rage lit inside of me. The set of my shoulders gave visible confirmation that I was not to be trifled with.

While we had discussed our options for returning with this Book of Knowledge, for completing our mission as directed, this latest stunt by the Council was tipping me away from letting anyone in a position of authority hold on to this much magick. We may not know fully what it contained, but if they wanted it so badly they would blow me up to get it, I was going to make the war a lot more deadly. I was tired of running. Tired of being a target for the Ferin. Of being jerked around by the Assembly. Tired of being tired. The tide was swinging, and I was about to hop a ride with it.

"Let's find a library," Jack said. "I have an idea."

Once again, looking like homeless refugees meandering the streets of the city, we searched for a library we had visited in the past. Gone. Not wanting to risk using his TC to find the data, Jack resorted to asking people we met, most of whom stared at us like we were five shades of crazy. Who uses a library anymore? Switching gears, we started looking for a cafe with internet access. Hopping on the world wide web was not ideal. Our network activity would be flagged the instant we asked the wrong question. Jack would need to be stealthy in his queries, finding the information through back doors and without being direct. No point in laying out breadcrumbs. The TC ensured the Assembly had ringside seats to the explosion. They knew we survived. Digging in my bag, I found the listening device the Ferin had buried in it. Temptation urged me to crush it under my heel and leave the parts scattered on the road, but a better thought came to mind.

"Good guys 462. Ferin 0. You lose." I dropped the bug back into the depths of my pack and swung it up on my shoulder.

Jack looked at me and grinned. He does love a good fight, and my jab guaranteed another round with the Ferin elite. It would take them some time to recruit another scout and gather up a squad, but I had faith they would find volunteers.

Tick tock.

It took two more blocks to find a place Jack deemed acceptable. Coffee and snacks to keep me satisfied and computers to rent by the hour. Reaching in my bag again, I pulled out my wallet, pleased to be back on Earth where my money meant something again. Picking out the biggest muffin and ordering the darkest espresso they could make, I settled into a padded chair and sighed in contentment. Jack smiled again, seeing me happy over the littlest pleasure. He took his coffee and began pecking away at the keyboard, the screens flashing and changing like a kaleidoscope on steroids. I had no chance of keeping up with the images flying past, so people-watching would be my morning hobby.

The coffeehouse itself was quiet, only three other people going about their day, reading the newspaper, sipping coffee or tea, unaware of the explosion that rocked the building only five blocks away. The news was not on the radio or TV station feeds yet, but it would. Then the chatter would ramp up. For now, it was peaceful. I savoured my drink and watched the taxis on the street; the people rushing this way or that, all with somewhere important to go. The clicking continued. Whatever trail Jack had found, he was furiously following it. Knowing he would give me the abbreviated version later, I finished up my snack and went to use the washroom to clean up. While our wayward appearance kept the locals from being too interested, it would not do to have them recall two people in the cafe that looked like someone had thrown them from a building.

Looking in the mirror, I saw fresh lines etched on my face. The pace and stress, the pressure of this mission were all being written for the world to see. The self-absorbed nature of most people keeps them from being concerned about what may be going on in someone else's life. We learn to keep ourselves to ourselves. I can appreciate that, especially at the moment. But it is very insular. As a species, we need to be communities of individuals working as one, not individuals working independently in the community. We have lost the sense of unity, of joint purpose, of brotherhood. Right now I could use some brotherhood. I thought I had found it in the Universal Guard. All of us selected for our unique talents, brought together to protect the Universe, to bring peace and harmony, order out of chaos. But I didn't see any of them protecting my back right now. Our boss and our enemy both know where we are. Yet, here we are, Jack and I, in a tiny shop on a tiny street in an enormous city, all alone on this big rock.

I let my mind wander as I cleared the grime from my skin. We had done damage to the Ferin, but the Council knew our mission and where we were expected to go. The smart money would be on ambushing us on our return to the Assembly hall. It would happen, eventually. The Ferin were not long on patience, but I could hope.

In the meantime, information absorbed from the Book was swirling around in my brain, little bits causing sparks of recollection, lighting up memories that had long lay dormant. Like dreams of places long unseen, they faded in and out, drifting through my thoughts like petals on a stream. Flickers of colour would catch my attention, then sink, some resurfacing, some catching on the edges and falling behind. Out of the corner of my eye, I saw the door open. A glint of metal was all I recognized before the needle hit home. Damn it! I felt my consciousness being pulled onward, the energy building, becoming more frantic, as the stream gained speed and rapids appeared. My metaphor morphed into an energetic reality, thoughts become real. As my attempts to grab onto any one solid image became hopeless, I collapsed to the floor. I was along for the ride, destination unknown.

Come back to me

“So, Ambassador. A little out of your depth, are we?”

My mind was swimming in molasses again. The voice and the face that went with it floated before me, the words more visible than the features. Finally having something to anchor to, I used my aura to reach for the speaker, needing the last of my dwindling energy to do so. I was so tired. Tired of running. And tired of hiding. Tired of being the good guy against an army of bad guys. Maybe this would be an enjoyable way to go. I mean, my reputation always listed me as the most likely to die of an overdose in a public place. Not really, but the humour of it woke me up a bit.

My body was truly laid out on a bathroom floor, somewhere out of reach. Pulling back some of my auric tendrils, I sent two out in search of my physical form. It might come in handy to plan a quick return route. While I did all that, another segment of my consciousness deduced the identity of my heckler: Elarenah.

“Princess,” I whispered, my voice sounding far away and dry

as dust. "How nice of you to invite me to tea once again. I would bow, but I don't seem to be quite myself at present."

Elarenah chuckled, her laughter rolling around me like bubbles. "I believe you would refuse my hospitality, were I to offer it to you." She probably had a point. The last tea party had not been a resounding success for either of us.

Understanding a little better where I was, I pulled myself together. Once you grasp the theory that energy is matter, then you can create matter out of any energy at hand. Here I could coalesce into any form I chose, appearing in any manner I wished. The fear of being lost in the cosmos abated as I focused on bringing the best parts of me to one place, leaving out the wrinkles and scars.

I was tempted to let my wings hang out for all to see. Elarenah no doubt knew about them. But, selfishly I guess, I just wasn't ready to be my true self for others, especially someone I didn't like all that much. Running through all of my options, I settled for just being me. It was, after all, my most familiar body. The odds of me getting into a fight in this realm were very slim. The odds of winning such a fight? Non-existent. My survival here was at Elarenah's mercy. I brought myself together and stood on wavering legs, the sensation of being upright making me slightly nauseous as my senses adjusted to life without a meat suit. Taking one more second to draw on the magick that built Otherworld, my thought processes clearing, I opted to see just how 'physical' I could make my structure become. The Fae who dwelt here did it. Why couldn't I?

In previous visits, I had done so as little more than a spirit, staying ethereal, never becoming solid. Things were different now. A faint memory stirred, the images shifting into focus as I considered whether or not I knew Otherworld better than I thought I did. I might not recall living here, but my soul did. Compared with my recent revelations, this question was one of far greater magnitude. Simply thinking of the possibility triggered an energetic response that had ley magick recreating my body. I watched as skin generated and bone solidified until I stood strong. I marvelled at the creation that was me, turning my hands over and back, smiling at the accomplishment.

"Ahem," the princess coughed gently. "If you are done admiring yourself?"

Not even the suggestion of surprise. I was still stunned it had worked, and she was all 'business as usual'. Still in awe, I followed Elarenah as she moved off into the trees lining the stream. Glancing about between moments of giddiness, I sensed eyes on us from other denizens of her world. I was still fiddling with my appearance as we entered a clearing. I clad myself in a renaissance style gown with flowing sleeves and gold trim. It wasn't practical, but it sure was pretty.

Elarenah arched an eyebrow when she saw what I was doing. Colour brightened my cheeks as I felt like a small child caught with her hand in the cookie jar.

"Come on, Elarenah," I badgered. "It's fun to play dress up!" I spun around to let the skirts twirl around me, small butterflies flitting up from the grass to dance with me.

The princess just stood and waited until I got it out of my system. Tiny titters from the treeline reminded me we were not alone. At least I amused the on-lookers, gave them stories to tell about the Guardian who had arrived in their midst.

"Do you have the Book with you?"

Elarenah's question stopped me cold. The Book. The Book that was linked to me, hidden within my body. A body that was passed out in a bathroom without my protection. Maybe even dead. I did not know what was in that shot. Shit! Panic was about to take over when Elarenah raised her delicate hand and halted my flight back to the stream.

"I should have asked 'Could you show me the Book?'"

"Why would that be any different?!" I cried. "I am here and the Book is there, trapped in my body!"

"Are you sure?" Elarenah's voice remained calm, rising delicately above the volume of the wind sighing in the trees.

I stopped, uncertain of what she was asking. How could the Book be here? Why would she think…?

I stood in the circle, blinking, not moving, as I processed the question again. Was I sure? In the aftermath of my anxiety, I felt a calmness grow in my belly. What if I did still have the Book? Was that even possible? I had held it so often I could recreate the density of it in my hands. Closing my eyes, I forced myself to breathe at a normal rate, focusing on the physicality of the Book of Knowledge. I dropped to the ground and placed my hands as if I were holding the Book in my lap. I imagined the sigils carved on the cover, the weight of the paper, the texture of the leather. And from the ether, the Book solidified.

The noises that surrounded us became ones of wonder. My eyes opened, fixed upon the Book which had appeared like the magick tome it was. Without a puzzle, without a key, without a challenge, the pages lay open before me, the ink as bright as the day the text was written. I traced the words, the letters and symbols once strange to me, now flowing as poetry and prose bringing tears to my eyes, the beauty of it so pure it was hard to look at.

I raised my face to gape at Elarenah, my astonishment obvious as I put the last piece in place. Hardly daring to believe it to be true, I closed the Book only to reopen it to read the bookplate.

It was in my handwriting. The name on the first page was not immediately familiar, as I had not used it in a millennium. It had taken a Fae princess and a quest through the galaxy to bring me back to what I once was. With this realization, the tears began in earnest. Tears for all I survived as Stephanie, tears for all I endured in the history of my soul, for losing my identity, and for the memory of a world I once held dear, long, long ago.

Darkness fell in Otherworld as I adjusted yet again to the new/old me. These breakdowns were making me question everything I thought to be true. They also went a long way to explaining why the Book felt so comfortable joining itself to me. The Book of Knowledge was priceless in what it contained, but the one who would value it the most would be its author. Much like a diary, the contents detailed the life and times of myself and those around me. Images and depictions of how we lived and worked, created and learned, and ultimately, how things all went wrong, all these and more rose before me. As I read each page, relived memory upon memory, the youngest Fae played around me, decorating my hair with blossoms, bringing me honey and small cookies to bolster my strength. Time slipped away, and the fireflies joined the children in joyous frivolity and laughter. The lightness of their actions, the carefree nature of their lives, made me miss the quietness of the forest life.

With a deep sigh, I pushed myself up off the ground, my legs damp with dew creeping up from the soil. I had been here long enough. I looked around for Elarenah; the princess having left me to my daydreams hours before. The children and fireflies scattered at my sudden movement, their squeals carrying through the quiet of the trees, giving me a path to follow.

Taking my book with me, I wandered beneath the heavy boughs, the stars barely visible between the leaf-laden branches. Night birds called as the gentle breeze carried the scent of roses to tickle my nose. Ahead of me stood a peaceful town with streets of cobblestone and simple houses. But the gardens. Even in the twilight, there were not enough words in the English language to describe the beauty. Moon-flowers opened to drink in the beams of light, while daylilies folded up their leaves for the night. I sat and pictured the riot of colour that would be present in daylight. A veritable feast for the eyes. I would miss Otherworld, no matter how brief this visit had been. To finish our mission, I needed to return to Earth. I had much to do to ensure the safety of this missive. And Jack must surely miss me by now.

Above me, standing on the balcony of her elegant home, Elarenah waved. I approached and stood looking up, seeing the wondrous night sky that framed her figure, the enormity of the galaxy, and the stars that twinkled in the crystalline air.

"It is time then," Elarenah said.

"It is," I responded. "I thank you for bringing me here. For bringing me to myself. I owe you."

A collective gasp rose as the residents watching us registered the favour I proffered to their ruler. This had not been done lightly. A debt such as this can only be repaid in kind. Elarenah dipped her head in acceptance. The day would come when she would reclaim it. I had to have faith the cost would be worth it.

"I have learned many fascinating things during my interactions with you. Not all great things to be sure, but I learned much about myself, and about those around me. And now I have learned who I am. What I am. And I know what I must do." That sounded like an impressive exit line to me, so I bowed to Elarenah and turned to walk from the town, leaving behind a shared journey and a delightful memory.

"Be careful who you trust, Witch. Things are not as you believe." Elarenah's voice carried through the night. "Look at those closest to you. There is deception."

And on that ominous note, the air about me thickened, blocking out the sky above, disguising the path and choking the breath from my lungs. Pushing against the black, I tried to resist the panic as darkness overtook me and I fell once more.

Ear worm

"STEPHANIE!"

I awoke to the sound of a door slamming open under the weight of Jack's body. Blinking to clear my vision, I sat up, my brain foggily grasped what had happened. Jack tripped over my legs, propelled forward in his haste to find me. Being in a tangle on a bathroom floor is not my idea of a good time. I was mentally exhausted from the journey. And Elarenah's last words hung in my mind. Doubt is a great eroder of trust. Jack seemed so grateful to find me alive and well if a little concerned about why he found me on the floor. I struggled with the thought of Jack betraying me. But he was the only one close to me. Ever. I had little contact with my fellow Guards or my Commanding Officer, having long ago given up friends of any kind.

Except for Jack.

Struggling to my feet, I refused his hand as I brushed myself off. Jack's eyes registered the hurt before doing the same. Uncertainty clouded the experience, and I couldn't talk about it. The sliver of doubt would grow and expand if I didn't dispel it. Fucking fairies.

While an entire day had passed in Otherworld, less than twenty minutes had ticked for Jack. He barely had time to notice my absence, yet I felt he should have done so sooner. It wasn't fair; I knew that, but I questioned what he was doing while I traversed realms. I wanted to share my experience, but could I trust him? We had been through some deep shit together, but this was on a completely different level. On one hand, he handled the entire wing thing without batting an eye. Who's to say he wouldn't handle the truth about my past? I mean, we all have one, right? We have all lived through things that our souls remember, even if we don't.

Only now, I remembered.

Now, I knew. Now, I was not just Stephanie, the Witch, the Ambassador, and the Guardian. With the remembering, with the trip to Otherworld, with the amalgamation of all I had learned, I regained my roots. A simple human existence would not be enough anymore. But first, I needed to figure out how to protect myself, protect the Book, and, if he was still worthy, protect Jack.

Walking without direction, I became lost in my thoughts. Where I would normally hold Jack's hand and exchange loving glances, Elarenah had gotten into my head. Keeping my hands stuffed into my pockets, I hunched my shoulders and simply walked. I warred within myself, my heart telling me to get over it, that she couldn't be right. But my mind kept going over the past few days, looking for signs of betrayal. I found nothing obvious. Our interactions had been normal. Well, as normal as they can be while being chased and blowing shit up.

I had trusted Jack for decades, over a century. He had been beside me, without fail, without thought for his own safety on more occasions than I could count. The idea of distrusting him cut me so deeply that Jack felt my conflict. Our years together gave him the wisdom to give me my space, but I sensed his confusion. He had done nothing wrong. He rushed to find me and I hadn't been decent enough to thank him. I had been a bitch ever since my venture into Otherworld and Jack deserved better.

Ultimately, my emotions over-ruled the doubts and I gave him the slightest smile to reassure him all would be well, that I just needed time to work some shit out. A mind-speak message would be clearer, but I slammed that door shut when I woke up and it would take time before I was comfortable letting Jack into my head again. I felt certain that some of his angst came from being locked out, but we would need a private place to discuss everything and soothe his feelings.

With an idea in mind, I turned to ask Jack if he knew of a nearby hotel. To my surprise, I stood alone. In my own little world, I had blocked out any connection to Jack, not realizing when he stopped. Looking back along our path, I tried not to get nervous about the people jostling me. I craned up on my tiptoes to look over the heads of the milling crowd before stepping into the doorway of a small shop, hoping to see Jack if he walked by. After several minutes with no sighting, I peered around the wall to see if he was standing on the sidewalk looking for me. Surely, he couldn't be that far behind. I may have been out of it, but Jack was always aware of his surroundings.

Deciding to retrace my steps, I made it two blocks before spotting him in a small alley.

"Jack!" I cried out. "Are you okay?" Looking past him, I saw a black car backing up. Jack pushed his sleeve down and stepped through the slight mist flowing across the ground. He appeared to be fine, even turned and waved at the car before coming to join me on the sidewalk.

"Sorry. I was so deep in thought I lost track of you." I said with a smile, encouraging him to fill me in.

"No problem," Jack replied, smiling back, still straightening his jacket.

"Someone you know?" I inquired, gesturing at the car nearly gone from our sight.

"Just needed directions." Jack turned and started walking again. "So where to next?"

I stood there, puzzled. Their conversation seemed more intimate than telling a stranger where to go. But Jack hadn't said it was a stranger. He avoided answering that part of the question. My misgivings kicked in again. Was I being paranoid because of Elarenah? Or was something going on? Jack often went off on his own when he did research work. No reason for the two of us to stare at the same screen. Before my over-active imagination took off again, I shook my head to dislodge any cobwebs and made a decision. We were going to talk about everything, without any bugs or devices or eavesdroppers. Time to come clean.

Choosing the first appropriate hotel on the street, I practically dragged Jack behind me, not trusting myself to go through with my plan, not trusting Jack to stay with me. The strange episode with the black car had started the voices up again, and I replayed the scene, trying to spot more details. When no additional information came up, I filed it away, having to place my faith somewhere.

Jack checked us in, selecting a room at the back, not on the ground floor, not so high up we could not jump out a window if it came to that. There are so many rules to consider when picking a safe house. Finding a lower-level room without bars on the windows was a plus. In New York City? Damn near impossible. The next best thing would be a small place with stairs to the rooftop. That we found. With Jack satisfied as to our defences and escape if necessary, I moved to the next big item on the list.

I paced the room, struggling to find a starting point. We would need to mind-speak our conversation. Nothing I was about to talk about, or ask, needed to be overheard by either the Assembly or the Council. Cutting down on our eavesdroppers, I tossed my bag and its bug into the shower and closed the door. Guessing we had about three hours before our visitors arrived, I took a deep breath.

'You know I love you, right?' Jack asked before I finished opening the link. His emotions poured through the gap, anxiety competing with worry and concern.

'I know,' I protested. *'I know. There is some shit I want to tell you, but something is going on that is getting in my way.'*

Jack looked perplexed. *'What are you talking about?'*

'The alley. That car. Whoever it was, they weren't asking for directions. You acted like you knew them. Why lie about it?' I continued pacing, uncertain which way to go next, uncertain I should have led with that question.

'I have no idea what you are talking about. What car?' Jack looked confused now, bordering on panic, his thoughts and brain waves echoing his words. He remembered nothing about the car or its occupants. Not good. Jack was being controlled somehow. He definitely met someone, they definitely spoke, and he definitely did not remember it. What the fuck was going on? What had Elarenah known that she did not tell me?

Jack's face reflected my thoughts just before I barricaded my mind again. Whoever had access to him could not gain access to me or we were screwed.

Kickin' it Old School

T ime to go old school. We couldn't talk about anything important until I found something to keep the bugs busy. Unfortunately, Jack had no idea what I was all freaked out about. And we couldn't use mind-speak until I knew who controlled Jack. Running through our options, I went digging around in the desk. I held up the pen and paper and raised a finger to my lips to keep Jack from asking anything else. As I sat down to write out my thoughts and ideas, Jack turned on the TV, choosing an obnoxious sitcom that filled the room with canned laughter every three minutes. This better not take long, or I was going to put my boot through the screen.

Reflecting on what I experienced while in Otherworld, I kept most of the journey to myself. There would be time to explain my actions later. For now, I needed to know what Jack had learned while I was passed out. Jack set out his notebook and his computer. Whatever he already recorded, the Assembly knew about, so there was no harm in reviewing it. Some information was trivial, brief mentions of a disappearing magickal book complete with a curse. Most of the records focused on the curse, of course. Drama always sells, and it is easier to remember. Grisly deaths seemed to follow all who wrote about the book or claimed to own it. It was well travelled, appearing in Egypt, India, England, even Central America. Details were sparse, describing it as being leather-bound and engraved with carvings and symbols. There was even a brief note about the interior in Merlin's writings. Trust a master magickian to glean some hint of what lay tucked between those decorated covers. He was mostly right, especially the part about the ancient, forgotten language, and he came close with the mention of Atlantis as its probable origin. Jack had copied the notes in their entirety without knowing their importance.

It was those same notes Madam found, hoping for a glimpse of the magnificence penned by Merlin. And those same descriptions had prompted the Assembly and the Council to go after the Book. Little did they know who they had sent to retrieve this particular piece of history. And I was not about to tell them.

Knock, knock, knock.

Seriously. Already? I looked at the time to see how long it had taken. Two hours, seventeen minutes. Someone was getting impatient.

After first glancing through the peephole, Jack opened the door to look at the tiny man standing there. His suit gave him away, as did his demeanour. The Assembly always hires well-dressed individuals to make their deliveries. Something about maintaining an image, words usually said while they glared at me sideways and tried not to grimace. I was not known for dressing up to appear before the Supreme Director and her colleagues.

Jack motioned for me to come to the door. The messenger had clearly been ordered to address me personally. The man extended a formal-looking envelope as he primly stated, "The Supreme Director requests your presence at the noted Gathering of the Assembly." Without waiting for my reply, he turned sharply on one heel and marched back down the hallway. The look on my face when I turned back to the room must have given away my consternation, for Jack arched that famous eyebrow of his in question.

"The Supreme Director requests your presence at the noted Gathering of the Assembly." I echoed, my voice slightly less prim and considerably more snippy when I said it. The envelope dropped to the table as I pursed my lips, thinking many other thoughts, none of them charitable. "Can't say it's a surprise. They did send us on this adventure after all. I'm sure they were expecting us back weeks ago." The level of annoyance increased with each statement, my attempts at raising my eyebrow still a failure.

Jack just grinned, knowing how little I like the politics and the arena they play in.

"So don't go," came his answer, as if it was that easy to decline a royal decree. While my future decisions might put a target on my back, I didn't need to increase the price tag beforehand.

Picking the envelope back up to open it, I read the invitation over twice before tossing it and its contents on the floor. I looked pointedly at Jack before going into the bathroom. "Can you please order some dinner? Like, lots of dinner?" I said as I turned on the shower. "I would like to eat before we go out."

Jack read the invitation before cursing. He has a very colourful vocabulary. I'm sure whoever was listening learned a few unfamiliar words. Deciding we deserved a decent meal, Jack ordered the best deal on the menu, then hollered back, "Thirty minutes or it's free!"

My stomach assumed a fantastic New York pizza would soon be on our doorstep. A loud grumble rose as I started daydreaming about all that grease and pepperoni. And bacon. I rushed the rest of my routine so Jack could have a turn. Waiting for our food, I took time to sort out what I needed to tell Jack, trying to be as quiet as I could, hiding my scribbling behind the nightly newscast.

"Hey, Jack. Did you hear about some explosion downtown this morning?" I asked sarcastically. We rarely witness the results of our handiwork. The newscaster detailed the property damage caused by the blast, an apparent gas leak being blamed once again. Big shock there. No fatalities, so that was a bright spot in the day. "Looks like a fireball ripped through some hotel."

Jack dried his hair with a small towel as he exited the bathroom, another wrapped around his waist. "You know, angel, you could have left me a larger towel."

I sat back and smirked. Jack couldn't care less about his towel size. And I, for one, enjoyed the view for an instant before the door was pounded on again.

This time I jumped up, the smell of the warm mozzarella and tomatoes drifting in clouds around the delivery man as he came down the hall. I barely remembered to scan the hallway before opening the door. I swear my stomach is going to get me killed one of these days.

After giving the guy a memorable tip, the two of us sat and devoured the food, checking the clock as we went. Time is quickly running out.

Return to the Hall

I would be giving away all the mysteries if I told you where we were going or how we got there. The Assembly location is one of the Universe's best-kept secrets, and I am not about to give that away. I am still an Ambassador and a Guardian after all. At least for the moment.

The hall always reminds me of the movie scene with the aliens and creatures of all types coming and going through the main entry point. The feeling of it being a vast airport terminal with destinations to star systems and galaxies beyond measure always makes me stop and admire the view. Each window, elegantly framed in ancient stone, peered out onto a world or space being monitored by the Assembly. As their influence had grown, so had the hall itself, now a sprawling edifice of glass and granite, coloured by the light of a million stars.

As we entered the Gathering, Jack brushed imaginary dirt from his sleeve while he casually glanced around at the seated members. I chose to check my weapons, adjust my shoulders, and made it clear I was preparing for a fight.

Supreme Director Childres motioned for me to step forward,

the guards moving to positions to prevent Jack from joining me, attempting to isolate me in the centre of the room. Enough of their games. I turned to each guard and glared. Each decided it would be unwise to lay hands on Jack, preferring to flank us on our trek. Shannon pursed her lips, clearly not liking the fact that her troops would be disobedient in front of her peers and my chain of command. The whispers began, softly at first, the volume increasing as those present asked questions, made comments, and gambled on the outcome. Trust any group to bring the baseline down to 'who's going to win?'

We kept our steps measured and calm, in no particular hurry to stand in the middle of this mass. While distant, there was enough magick in this room to do a nova-style execution without blinking. Only the wards, placed in layers by master magickians, and the honour system instituted by past Assemblies, gave me confidence they would wield no magick against us. It also gave me the freedom I needed as I felt for the pulsing ley lines beneath us, the crossroads just ahead, conveniently buried below the platform we were about to step on.

"Ambassador DuMonde, have you brought the Book of Knowledge as requested?" Director Childres dismissed any use of a microphone, her voice ringing through the hall like church bells.

"Hello, Madam Director. I'm fine, thank you for asking. I hope you are well." Okay, maybe it shouldn't have been my opening line, but I do like manners, and I don't like being bullied. The whispers increased, and the overall chatter included a chuckle or two at my insolence.

The Supreme Director tightened her face another notch, not appreciating my humour, nor the appearance I had created—that she didn't care about her Ambassadors, only in results. It does not go well to make your people uneasy about your commitment to them.

"And, no. I have not brought you the Book." My clear voice, amplified to carry smoothly over the crowd, created yet another wave of noise as the Assembly commented on my audacity to defy the order. Now the bets flew in earnest. I got the sense the odds were weighted heavily against me. I could cash in if someone wanted to take my chit.

The Supreme Director picked up her gavel and pounded it on the table before her to regain control. Peering down from her perch, Shannon Childres gave us the coldest stare I have seen in a long time. Years ago, I would have withered under her gaze. Not now. Not today. As I stood before her, unwavering in my position or my expression, the Supreme Director was in an awkward position of her own. In this game of chicken, she had the most to lose, and she would not go down easily.

Standing at ease beside me, Jack winked at Director Childres. His spunk made my mouth twitch as I attempted to contain the smile threatening to break out across my face. It was so hard to stay serious with him next to me, making eyes at the Supreme Director. We had agreed in advance not to use mind-speak as we did not want any attraction drawn to that ability, or pick up any hitchhikers able to read our thoughts. With the possibility of powerful magickians surrounding us, it was not an acceptable risk.

Her scrutiny made the members uncomfortable, and I heard the rustling of people adjusting in their seats, the murmuring taking on a new tone. Director Childres heard it as well and, like any adept politician, she knew when to concede a point. She sat back in her chair and relaxed, a signal to the masses to calm down. Nothing happening here.

Removing her glasses, the Supreme Director tapped them gently on her armrest, using the quiet, steady rhythm to gain everyone's attention where the gavel would have been heavy-handed. Point to Director Childres. The chatter in the room gradually decreased, and the members inched forward in their chairs, straining to hear what came next.

I turned on the spot, looking at each director as I circled the hall, making eye contact with most. Two empty seats made me wonder who else had defied the Supreme Director. I grinned widely and rolled my shoulders as I turned back to face Director Childres.

I had always been a fan of the old west. The swagger of the gunmen as they approached their duel. Their dusters like medieval cloaks on knights of old. The dramatic flair when they flung their coattails back to reveal their holsters. This entire scene reminded me of that. I really wanted to be wearing a duster. Or a cloak.

Jack shuffled slightly away from my side, assuming his at-ease position as though there was nothing to see here. Sleight of hand is mostly about what you want people to look at, using distraction to mask what you don't want them to see. With each movement he made, the focus of the Assembly shifted to follow him, wondering what he would do. Or just to watch him move. He is a marvellous piece of eye candy, after all. I chuckled, thinking about that for a second. Jack shot me a look, and I returned it with a sultry one of my own, turning up the heat a bit.

As I stood before the Supreme Director and debated my options, Jack shivered as though an icy wind had swept over him. Childres smirked, her face creased in the unnatural shape. A part of me wondered what she had to be pleased about. The rest of my brain was more interested in finding a way out of this mess. Glancing at Jack, a niggle of concern poked at me. His movements were distracting as he stepped forward three paces, then turned back for four. He was erratically working his way around me, the sputtering method making me worried. The murmuring rose among the directors. Deciding Jack had his own methods and means, I concentrated on the Supreme Director and what was about to happen.

"Ambassador Stephanie Alecretia DuMonde. You are hereby ordered to surrender the Book of Knowledge to the Assembly as a whole and to the Supreme Director for safekeeping and containment."

The decree, read aloud by my Commanding Officer, General Mathers, held the weight of military reprisal for disobedience.

Director Childres wasn't pulling any punches now. It was one thing to be insolent, another to be insubordinate. I reluctantly stepped forward to address the General, snapping to attention as I did so, expecting Jack to fall in on my rear.

Instead, he remained off to the side, and I looked quizzically over my shoulder at him. It was not like Jack to back down. Or to leave me exposed like this. He continued circling in his odd way, staying well away from me and the package I carried, muttering as he went. From the sounds of the words drifting back to me, he was arguing with himself.

The Supreme Director's smile widened, reminding me of the Cheshire Cat, and settled back into her chair, arrogance blooming on her age-worn face, surety in her eyes. General Mathers took a single step down the stone staircase, still as stoic as ever, yet the quickness in his motion had me looking about to select which enemy to prepare for first.

As the General extended his hand, anticipating my complete compliance with his directive, I looked at Jack again, growing concerned about his lack of response to the perception of a threat against us. His stature and the slump of his shoulders gave me pause. I turned to him, and for the first time, arched an eyebrow in question. His eyes were a curious shade of blue, almost cloudy. There was definitely something wrong.

Broken

"They told me you never truly loved me." The words came from Jack in a breathless, painful gasp, barely audible yet harsh enough to cut through to my heart.

"They told me you only used me for my brain, and maybe my body. That none of it was real. That no one could love a monster like me." Jack's face showed the strain of his internal struggle, his mouth saying words his heart never would.

"They told me you would never listen to them, that you wanted to keep the power, that you never intended to share it." Jack slowly turned away from me, addressing the Assembly rather than face me directly. His presence and his aura projected the abject grief he felt saying these things. The directors angled forward in their seats, hanging on every word, tasting the betrayal cutting through the air as he spoke.

Nothing else done here, no comments or orders had moved me. This might. I would have to give up the Book to prove him wrong. The words hit me as they arced through the space between us, space that grew with every step he took. Like blows to the stomach, they took my breath away and threatened to bring me to my knees, the pain of the loss sinking in, bit by bit. How could Jack believe such things? After all we had survived together. After everything we meant to each other. How could he....

"They told me there was a cure in the Book. A cure for my condition." Back where he started, Jack spun around to face me. "A cure you would not give me!" His voice broke under the tension, hands clenched until his knuckles grew white.

"After all the searching, the answers are right there. And I can't get to them while you keep the knowledge to yourself!" Jack stepped towards me, and for a moment, I considered stepping back. But I could not, would not, be afraid of this man. He may have just broken my heart into five million shards of glass, but I would not step away from him.

Like sharks circling in the water, the directors were practically dancing on their tiptoes, waiting for the final blow in a title fight. The Supreme Director rose to her feet, crossing her arms in front of her like the end was already written. I only needed to lay down my 'sword' and then fall on it.

Jack lifted his gaze to face me, watching the tears once again streaming down my face, his words damaging me in ways nothing else could.

"They told me you would never stay with someone like me," he hissed. "That our years together meant nothing to you!"

My heart, battered and bruised, felt like it would never be

whole, yet when I looked him in the eye, the truth became clear. Within him, war raged. The images flickered in his eyes, the conflict between what he uttered and his intent, his truest self revealed in the shadows playing across his face. Reaching beyond the words, beyond the actions, beyond the initial perception, I looked. And then I saw, deep in the corner of my peripheral vision, the tiniest thread of magick extending from the TC on Jack's wrist to his arm and embedding itself into his skin.

There, at that moment, in that sliver of time, I finally had enough pieces. They slipped into place like a slow-motion segment of a movie, clicking as they solidified. And at that moment, standing there, within the silence, I understood, and I made my choice.

Trusting in my intuition over the hurt, I raised my hand and held it out for Jack to take. I wanted to see for myself, feel for myself, the true nature of what he was being forced to do. If they had complete control, he would ignore me and walk away. If the programming had not beaten down every last vestige of who he was, Jack would take my hand and I would have access to the person I believed was feeding him this line of crap.

General Mathers was also approaching, no longer confident that I intended to obey his order. His march to the floor of the chamber would take several seconds, time I did not have to spare as I implored Jack to hold my hand. The struggle was very real. His mind was fighting against the directives implanted there, maybe yesterday, maybe months ago. Jack's hands flew up to grab the sides of his head as he stumbled, his resistance causing obvious distress and pain.

I shifted my eyes back and forth between Jack and the General, gauging who would make it to me first. The entire Assembly stood above us, their anticipation adding to the energetic storm swirling through the hall, filling the lofty ceiling with whirlwinds of emotion. Director Childres planted both hands on the bench before her, leaning forward as though she too could reach me.

Beneath his breath, Jack managed to exhale. "They told me…. lots of…… bullshit…..in the hopes…… that I would……. turn against… you… too." Screams of pain tore from his throat, agony ripping apart my heart even as my brain processed what he had said. The words, so quietly said as to be a secret between us, were all I needed to run to him and take hold of his arm. The members erupted in anger as I grabbed Jack at the moment of his collapse. With blood pooling under his nose from the cranial pressure, Jack whispered one last word before passing out on the cold ceramic tiles.

"Circle."

Magick for the Win

y eyes widened as I finally realized the reason for Jack's unusual walking pattern. Glancing at the General, I saw him pick up the pace, sensed the growing agitation among the directors and winced under the intense fury from the Supreme Director. But my focus centred on the tiles. Jack had set the circle with intention. Now, it only needed my magick to activate it. General Mathers, uncertain of my intent, broke into a run as I sprung up from the floor where Jack lay bleeding. Against my nature, I left him to make the only play remaining in the game.

Closing my eyes, I searched for the imprint in my mind that would show me the impression Jack had made in the energy field. Using magick in the Assembly hall is forbidden, as are so many other things. But, since someone invoked an influence spell on Jack, I felt justified in slapping my bloodied hand on his footprints, infusing them with his blood and the magick pooled within me. Fuelled by anger, the circle flared to life, a visible conflagration that gave off enough heat to drive the General back, putting an abrupt end to his advancement.

The crowd erupted in their own manner, their frustration at

having been denied an emotional feast adding to the storm brewing above us. Director Childres yelled to the guards, directing them to enter the circle, to break it by any means available. Good luck to them. I was not responsible for the ensuing carnage as they attempted to dispel the incantation and snuff out the flames.

Safe for the moment, I returned to Jack and the much more immediate problem. The TC still fed him the programming it was designed to do. With Jack unconscious, I struggled to analyze its effects. I was lost. Removing the device might kill him. Leaving it there might, too. Separating the TC from the ley line energy it projected seemed like my only option, but the line was deeply embedded, not only into Jack's skin, but piped directly into his brain. Like being hard-wired to life support, the energy might be attached to any part of him; his emotions, his memories, his central nervous system. Pulling the plug could literally pull his internal wiring apart. Hoping my guides and angels could help guide me, I found my pathway to the Universe blocked. So there was a Master Magickian in the house. Fuck. My intuition would have to be enough. Praying I was on the right track, I bent to take another look at the magick woven into him.

Relief swept over me as Jack stirred. Wiping the blood from his face, his clear eyes confirmed he had battled against their program and won. There may be damage to uncover, but as he struggled to his feet, Jack ripped the TC from his wrist. Looking squarely at Director Childres, he dropped the unit to the floor. A smile curled his lip. With as much effort and deliberation as he could muster, Jack lifted his size twelve boot and slammed it down on top of the computer, crushing it and severing the last link to his psyche.

Supreme Director Childres' face became a mottled mix of reds and purples, her eyes flashing with a rage seldom seen in a human. I had breached so many rules I would never again be allowed back inside the Assembly walls. And you know what? After struggling to earn the privilege, without my rose-coloured glasses, I didn't give a fuck if I never saw any of them again. From being a brotherhood and a cause I believed in, people I thought had my back and would be there when shit hit the fan… When all that happened, there was a complete and absolute dismissal from my brothers-in-arms, the Guard standing in a ring around the hall, ignoring one of their own. I knew then that I had not truly been one of them.

That I had always been an outsider.

That I had always stood alone.

Only now did I see that in being alone, I could find out who, and what, was most important to me. My life may have had a purpose, running about the Universe, believing I was working to protect the people within it. Now, I stood looking at the man who remained beside me, trustworthy despite all the manipulative tricks the Assembly had tried, all that they had pushed him through. I mean, I really looked at Jack. Then with a smile of my own, I took his hand in mine, saluted the Supreme Director and my Commanding Officer with a single finger, and promptly winked us out of the most heavily warded facility I had ever been in.

One Problem Solved

"Thank you, Your Highness," I bowed to our protector, supplicating before the Faerie leader who had given me the key to the wards. When we met on her planet, I held the power. Now, I was without a legion behind me, a warrior without an army.

"Witch," the Princess said as she tipped her head briefly before turning to walk away, the implication being that we should follow in her footsteps.

Jack was still trying to figure out whether or not we were going to kill the Fae. He swung his head back and forth between us, gauging the threat level, obviously confused at the turn of events.

Until this very point, I could not share my plan. With Jack being under an external influence and my sense of the wrongness of it had prevented me from revealing any part of my exit strategy. I had guessed he was being monitored, though I underestimated the extent of control Director Childres would try to exert. He had a long way to go to deprogram, but I felt confident he would make it. If I had harboured any doubts, I would have left him bleeding in the hall, answering questions about where I had gone, possibly being tortured. If I doubted my love for him and of his love for me, I would have turned my back and left him to that fate. Without the TC and its tendrils of magick being force-fed into him, Jack would soon be himself again, but would he be free of the doubts planted deep in his mind?

I stopped for a moment, turned to Jack and looked him straight in the eye. Nothing short of direct and total honesty would make this acceptable.

"Jack. I'm sorry I could not tell you sooner. Elarenah believed you were being monitored by the Supreme Director. She saw signs I could not." I paced about, trying to find the right words. "Even we did not guess the extent to which they would go. I know you felt the distance growing between us, and I know I hurt you because I could not tell you my suspicions. Can you forgive me?"

Jack, still uncertain where we were, how we got there, and why we were dealing with the two-faced Faerie princess, looked at me with more questions than answers on his face. With a shake of his head, he let the thoughts and ideas settle, then took my hand.

"My dearest angel, we have a lot to talk about. And to share." These simple words melted the last tendrils of fear from around my heart. "You need to know this: I will always love you. It doesn't matter what happened. Or what you are. It only matters that you believed in me. So, yes. I forgive you." Jack stooped to give me the gentlest of kisses, sealing his promise.

As the rays of the sun slowly faded into darkness, Jack pulled me close. Pushing the rest of the world away, we stood in comfortable silence beneath the stars. For the first time in years, the battle between good and evil in the Universe was someone else's problem.

"Now then, Lady Azarathe," came the haughty voice of the princess, interrupting us once again. "What do you plan to do about the Ferin?"

About the Author

Lisa VanGalen writes a mix of paranormal, mystery, thriller, and fantasy stories. A married mother with two grown sons, her days are now filled with wrestling words into submission and making sure the family dogs are fed.

You can connect with me on:

http://www.mystic-dragon-divination.ca/l-m-vangalen-author

https://www.facebook.com/LMVanGalen-Author-11267375715543

www.ingramcontent.com/pod-product-compliance
Lightning Source LLC
Chambersburg PA
CBHW071428200726
48294CB00002B/560